Gus Moreno

GUS MORENO
This Thing Between Us

Gus Moreno's stories have appeared in *Aure-alis*, *PseudoPod*, *Bluestem* magazine, and the anthology *Burnt Tongues*. He lives in the suburbs with his wife and dogs, but never think that he's not from Chicago.

THIS THING BETWEEN US

GUS MORENO

THIS THING BETWEEN US

MCD × FSG Originals
Farrar, Straus and Giroux
120 Broadway, New York 10271

Library of Congress Cataloging-in-Publication Data
Names: Moreno, Gus, 1985– author.
Title: This thing between us : a novel / Gus Moreno.
Description: First edition. | New York : MCD × FSG Originals /
    Farrar, Straus and Giroux, 2021.
Identifiers: LCCN 2021019887 | ISBN 9780374539238 (paperback)
Subjects: LCSH: Widowers—Fiction. | Technology—Fiction. |
    GSAFD: Horror fiction. | Suspense fiction.
Classification: LCC PS3613.O717567 T48 2021 | DDC 813/.6—dc23
LC record available at https://lccn.loc.gov/2021019887

Designed by Abby Kagan

Our books may be purchased in bulk for promotional, educational, or
business use. Please contact your local bookseller or the Macmillan
Corporate and Premium Sales Department at 1-800-221-7945, extension
5442, or by email at MacmillanSpecialMarkets@macmillan.com.

www.fsgoriginals.com • www.fsgbooks.com
Follow us on Twitter, Facebook, and Instagram at @fsgoriginals

7   9   10   8

To my wife, Monse

and

my sister-in-law, Carol

I.

Your parents wouldn't let me bury you in a tree pod. Mostly your mom.

After the groundskeepers backed a truck onto the grass and poured the rest of the dirt onto your grave, the funeral director let everyone know services were now over, and invited them to the potluck dinner we were having at your aunt's house.

My hands were covering my face. I could feel people walking past me to their cars. I didn't want to say goodbye or thank you, or listen to whatever they had to say. Between my fingers I saw the dewy grass glistening around my scuffed dress shoes. Someone squeezed my shoulder and said into my ear, "Thiago, what do you want us to do about the flowers?"

I pulled my face out of my hands.

Propped along one side of your brand-new plot were flower arrangements hooked on metal stands. One from your job, one from your cousins in Mexico who couldn't make it out so soon. They were originally delivered to the church, but people took it upon themselves to grab the arrangements and load them into their cars as they headed to the cemetery. And now, should they come back with us to your aunt's house for the potluck, or stay here?

The crowd had thinned out except for a few friends and family. News cameras stayed on the opposite side of the lot, their idea of respecting our privacy while they filmed. Everyone waited for me to do something. Standing around like cows in a field. No one looking at anyone.

Someone behind me said didn't the flowers usually stay.

"Okay," I said. "So we just leave them here."

Kris said the wind would blow the stands over.

"Take them off then," I said.

But, your mom said, the groundskeepers still needed to bring the machine over to flatten the fresh soil.

But, your cousin said, didn't the undertaker say they finished that?

The husband of one of your coworkers walked across a paved path to the next section of grass and tombstones and asked the group of guys wearing coveralls if we needed to wait for the soil machine, or if it was ever coming. People started pulling arrangements off the stands. Some bouquets weren't hooked on, they were just tied together.

People took off the flowers one by one and laid them on the grave.

"Wait," I said, but some of them spoke only Spanish and kept laying flowers. Angel had to translate for me, which confused the hell out of your aunts and uncles because she was Black.

It occurred to me that I couldn't go back to crying because I had to pee, which who knew peeing could outrank grief in the brain. We were all standing around like the cover to some Christian rock album. I could see in your family's body language that they felt uncomfortable not being allowed to lay flowers down when there were flowers to be laid, and why would we drive flowers to your aunt's house when tomorrow they would just end up in her trash, or compost.

I forget which one of your aunts was the gardener—the one who gave us a basket of tomatoes for our wedding as a gift, and we just laughed and threw them at the bridal party in the hotel parking lot—was it Tía Chiquis? Who we secretly called Tía Cheeky? Who didn't find it all that funny when I spelled her name that way in a birthday card we gave her, only because you dared me.

Your coworker's husband returned and said we could lay the flowers down. I was already holding the flowers people had laid down on your grave before we knew what to do with them, and now I went back to them like, you can lay these down, but they were already in the act of taking more flowers off the stands, so I was just standing there with my arms full of roses and tulips. Your mom took a couple and stuck the stems into the dirt. More people followed her lead. I couldn't remember whose car I rode in.

I didn't fight Diane on the funeral services, even after I told her we had already talked about it and neither of us wanted to be buried. Me and you hashed it out during one of those late-night talks couples have in bed, right before they fall asleep, or after sex.

Sex for us. I didn't tell Diane that part either.

Talking in the dark, limbs stacked together, two rhythms of breathing and a sheen that made our skin as glossy as a lingerie commercial.

We talked about getting cremated and the surviving one jumping out of a plane and opening the urn only to have it fly back up into the engine. Or we could shoot the ashes off into space. I worried about the carbon footprint cremation left on the world, so you brought up other options like that facility where they freeze the body in a drum and then sound waves batter the blue corpse until it shatters into a million pieces, T-1000 style.

It was all about being responsible with the body we'd leave behind, like washing our cups and cake plates at the end of a party. It was easy to hypothetically donate our corpses to a class of medical school students. My luck, the kid standing over me would be studying cosmetic surgery and I end up with a nice rack. You laughed. It was easy. We assumed death was a long ways off, or that it would gradually come into our lives and we would face it together.

Weeks passed and then you tagged me in a video for this tree pod burial thing. "THIS," you commented next to my name. The animated video showed how they placed the body in an egg-shaped capsule made of a biodegradable shell, planted a baby tree over that egg, and then filled the rest of the hole with dirt. The tree would grow and its roots would lengthen until they reached the egg, where they would leach off the body, turning it into food.

"A casket is such a waste," you said from the back seat of our car, scrolling through your phone as I drove. It was one of those perfectly timed occasions where I had dropped off a Lyft fare downtown and you happened to be getting out of work, so I scooped you up and headed home. "They're so expensive."

"So you want to live on as a tree?" I said.

Through the rearview mirror, you gave me what you called your Michelle Tanner not-amused look.

The whole business of you sitting in the back seat was part of our impromptu role-playing game, where I was Tom Branson, the Irish chauffeur from your favorite show, and you were the insufferable dowager countess of the Crawley family. "Westward, Branson . . ." "Change lanes, Branson . . ." "You're making me late, Branson." You in the power suit you looked poured into, telling me I was being ridiculous with only your eyes.

"Do you see a giant crystal hanging off my necklace, Thiago?" you said. "Is 'Namaste' tattooed on my wrist? I just like the idea of my body being completely recycled. It's a clean circle of tidiness. I think it's satisfying the part of me that always wanted a Trapper Keeper growing up. Now, southward, Branson."

"Yes, my lady," and me trying not to sound too excited as I turned onto the entrance ramp, eager to get you home.

When I told Diane about the tree pod, she took it like I suggested we take you to a taxidermist and have him glue leaves to your fingers. She had already been putting money down on a burial plot next to her parents for when she passed away. Guess your stepdad was shit out of luck. Guess the way she saw it, death meant they could finally go their separate ways, the contract fulfilled. Till death do us *part*, honey.

She put your body into her plot and started paying for the next one over so she could be buried next to you. And she gave you the big Catholic mass you always never wanted. The priest doing his best to spin you as a child of God because we never went to church and even passed on having a priest officiate our wedding. Remember what you told me when I dragged you to a screening of *The Seventh Seal*? "I just don't think about it," you said. "We die and that's the end. No heaven. No hell. Do not collect two hundred dollars."

Burying you in anything but an expensive casket set Diane's teeth on edge. What would telling her your thoughts on heaven and hell accomplish? I was trying to think like you, the way you navigated your mom's feelings for when the fight was actually worth it. So, your body sat in a casket in front of an altar, for a bunch of people who didn't matter to gawk at and pray over. My only condition was that I pay for all of it.

At the back of the church was a remembrance book where people wrote their goodbyes and condolences. I flipped through the pages as people filled the pews. Sometimes they stopped and pulled me into an embrace, assuring me we'd met before when they saw the stunned look in my eyes.

In the book, people left messages for me and for your parents. Some of them I did know. Hector, Bianca, Faust, and Lucy. Deidre hugged me and then wiped the tears off my lapel. She introduced me to her sister, saying, "This is my friend Thiago." *My* friend. Before they were *my* friends they were *your* friends. The longest friendship I had before meeting you was with a leather jacket.

"My deepest condolences," her sister said. "I can't imagine how painful this must be for you."

Yes, she could. They all thought they could, but they just didn't want to admit it. People cannot bear to think there are channels of human experience that are closed off to them, that they'll never know. People want to believe their experience is universal, that nothing's outside their scope. That their simulation of losing their spouse is just the same as my real loss.

I could see it when I caught them looking at me. Wondering how it would be for them.

What they say: call me.

What they mean: it's your responsibility to let me know when I have to care.

Someone with your maiden name had written a message in the book, and right below it was the squiggly handwriting of a child. It clicked in my head that this was your cousin. *That* cousin. The one whose two boys both had sunken Richard Ramirez eyes. It looked like the oldest one was forced to write something. He wrote, "Sory tio and tia that Vera died but life is life."

It was like he reached into my head and turned off the spigot. Instead of wiping away tears, I was laughing. I was gripping the back of the pew. *Life is life.* You had to be so inexperienced and emotionally dulled by YouTube channels to point out such an obvious truth and not recognize the lack of sympathy that went into it. At a wake. Leaving it for the parents and husband of the deceased to read.

I knew right away it would have been the thing we'd have said to each other as a joke if we'd read it at someone else's wake. Life is life. If one of us overdrew from our account. Life is life. If your mom begged you to visit her and then spent the whole time criticizing you. Life is life. If you missed the train and your phone died. Life is life. Shorthand for Shit happens, get over it.

It was the kind of empty saying people shared on social media, and if I had seen it there first it wouldn't have registered with me, but to see it in the book triggered something. I could barely breathe. The blood was heating under my face. I could feel my chest bouncing from the suppressed laughs. People were turning around. From the front pew, Diane stood up and peeked down the aisle.

Even with you in the news, on television, your photo in countless think pieces, this kid was walking around totally unaffected by it, which meant the world at large still turned without knowing your name. Without knowing your love of amortization calendars and kettlebells and the burned cheese parts sticking out of the end of a quesadilla. There was kind of a comfort in that obscurity. Regardless of how it felt now, the world would sooner or later have its foot on the gas pedal, on to the next bombing, the next shooting, the latest outrage, and we'd be forgotten. No more interview requests. No more private messages from strangers asking me to watch the tribute video they made of you. No more having to watch what I said when someone shoved their phone in my face. We'd finally be left to ourselves.

But seriously fuck that kid.

I figured you'd want your mom not to hate me more than you'd care how you were buried, so I gave her no push-back. I emailed her all the photos I had of you because she needed a recent one for the marble burial marker. It would say your name, and beneath that, *Loving Daughter, Cherished Wife*. And below that, *Until We Meet Again*.

Mourners crowded around the tables of food in your aunt's house, making their plates. As with every family event, packs of children were running through the house. I could hear them from the yard, running and laughing and get-ting yelled at to stop. Your friend Olivia rounded the cor-ner with a plate of food and found me sitting on the back steps.

"Hungry?"

I raised the beer to show her I was in the middle of something. She asked if that was from Terrence, because he was inside with two beers and looking for me.

So this was going to be the next step. Your friends all trying to furl me into their group, me functioning as your stand-in.

More of them filed out into the yard, thinking this

was acceptable, because why on earth would I want to be alone. Let the older folks stay inside while the cool kids hang with the widower. An impromptu storytelling session happened. One by one they shared stories of you, personal experiences, from your time at the University of Chicago, the monthlong friends trip through Europe, the late-night phone calls, the so many times you talked one of them off a ledge without you knowing it. All memories of just you and them, round after round of claims made on you, their memories of you. And when it got to me and I kept the beer up to my lips for an uncomfortably long time, they skipped over me and continued.

One story was about how elbowy you got on the dance floor if strangers moved too close. "Vera loved dancing," someone behind me said. "That was so her."

I wanted to swing my beer around and smash the bottle on whoever's face. You loved dancing, but you weren't some EDM kid thrusting the air in your purple leotard and blowing a neon whistle every weekend.

Did they know about the emotional scarring U of C left you with? Did they even notice how much you hated traveling with some of these "friends," because all they wanted to do was go clubbing through Europe, and all you wanted was to eat street food and hit as many churches and museums as you could?

They were so quick to define you, to pin you down to something. Who didn't like music? What dead person didn't have a great smile? A great laugh? No one was calling you these things when you were alive. Alive, you got to be just you. Dead, they needed to encapsulate you, harness you into a favorite movie they could buy, a favorite motto they could tattoo. No one got that you were those things primarily because you were you, not because they made you.

We never lined up on any of that kind of stuff. I went to a community college, hated dancing, and spent the least amount of time and effort needed to still be able to call people my friends. But we still worked together somehow, like two different animals that learned to hunt as a team. You were you and I was me and there was this thing between us.

What about this hasn't been seen in a billion other people? When haven't these feelings cycled through another person, from a loss just like this? When haven't men collapsed to their knees on crisp cemetery grass and belted out big throaty *Godfather III* sobs?

These feelings weren't new to the world, but that didn't stop it from feeling like they were. These same friends would later text me a line from some book or a quote from a movie that was supposed to comfort me, atheist friends messaging me about unexplained phenomena in physics and quantum mechanics that were supposed to prove how no one knew what anything meant. Bob Dylan lyrics. Books on reincarnation. *You have to listen to this song, Thiago. It'll help.* And sure, I could hang platitudes and facts on myself like ornaments, but it still didn't help. So what if the universe was a hologram? So what if this was all in our heads? The points being made never stuck. I couldn't synthesize this knowledge, but even worse, I couldn't even regurgitate it to at least convince myself I knew something about life, or death, or meaning. Something inherent. Something irreducible. With every moment the floor shifted under my feet. The world was pressed against my nose, too close to see. I had no story to follow. My favorite character was gone.

The hours ticked into the double digits and back into singles. Most of the guests were gone except a core group of friends and cousins who were still drinking and dancing in the basement. If it was one of them who'd died, they reasoned, Vera would have been on the dance floor all night. The nauseous green basement tile was now a dance floor. House music was pumping out of an Itza your aunt kept in the kitchen. They plugged it in downstairs and asked Itza to play Green Velvet and formed a circle, dancing in their black suits and skirts, hugging the wood-paneled walls, their heels getting caught in the grout.

White light spun around Itza's orb shape, the teeth-kicking bass to "Flash" started to pump into the basement, and my palms began to sweat from thinking about the time we did ecstasy and this song played.

"I can see the music," you said, playing with your fingers, waving them in front of your face.

"Me too," I said. "The bass is making me have to take a shit."

One of your friends, the one with purple highlights, opened the circle and waved me in. They all did. I waved them off. Something was receding within me. Beer was caking to my tongue.

My thoughts synced with the beat of the music. Drums cracked, and projected on the screen in my head was this: She's gone, she's gone, she's gone. I could feel your absence like a pulse running up and down the right side of my body where you were supposed to be sitting, your head on my shoulder.

The circle cheered and opened again when they saw me get up and walk toward them, but quieted down as I kept walking, heading up the stairs.

A silver lining to your death: I didn't have to feel things anymore. Your friends' feelings in that moment did not register on any level. That part of my life was over. The part that could care for another person, invest in them, it froze and then sheared off like a glacier, into the dead ocean of things I couldn't access anymore. It felt like freedom, actually.

I stepped outside through the side door where cars lined the driveway. It was blinding how black the sky was. The block was lifeless, dark windows and silence except for the muffled hum of music coming from the basement.

A man named Artie and his Toyota Camry were ten minutes away. I put my phone in my pocket and headed to the backyard because I knew there was a cooler next to the garage, and I wanted to get another beer while I waited. That was how I found your mom.

She was behind the house, standing in the yard with her back to me. She cleared her throat and leaned over to spit, a dribble snapping off the loogie and hanging from her lower lip. A small patch of grass was tamped down next to her feet, where the remains of her lunch were sitting.

Something kept me from walking to her, calling out to her. Your stepdad was either passed out in the house or he was gone. I stopped and watched and once she'd gotten that out of her system she straightened back up and returned to dancing. She was using the muffled beat from the basement as her music. Her right arm wrapped around an invisible partner's shoulder. The other arm straightened out in front of her. Instead of the invisible partner's hand inside hers, it was a plastic cup of sangria.

Her heels stabbed the lawn and popped out. She staggered side to side, mumbling her own song, the mumbles congealing into lyrics, words, barely above babbling but enough for me to understand she was trying to talk to someone, or at least thinking in her mind she was having a conversation. She alternated between giggling and sucking back snot, mumbling like a spanked child. Today was the first time I'd ever seen her out of that beige leather jacket she always wore, cut like a satin baseball jacket, the one thing of her father's her mother didn't donate when he died. In her family it was supposed to be the men who died young. Heart attacks, kidney problems, grinding their bodies to mud for a living. Not something as violent and unpredictable as what happened to you.

I never went for the beer. I watched from the shadow of the house until I got a notification my driver was out front. If Artie had looked into the back seat and asked why I didn't go to Diane, I probably would have said something about her being a hard-ass. She wouldn't have wanted people to see her like that.

But in writing about that night, the bullshit falls away. Truth was, I was embarrassed for her. Everyone around me was falling apart. Some version of those inflatable arm-waving tube-men car dealerships always have. I watched Diane and saw at least another hour of sitting with her in the kitchen, filling her with coffee. A long conversation about you. And I didn't feel like going through that. It was too much. I thought I could count on her to punch down her feelings long enough to break down on her own time, away from other people, like an adult.

Your mom wanted me to move in with them. I could sleep on the couch if I wanted.

Olivia and Terrence offered their spare bedroom.

Your friends called daily. The logic was that I shouldn't be alone the week after your burial.

They say tragedies like this bring people together. They're right. And it's suffocating.

I kindly swatted away the invitations. More human interaction was the last thing I wanted. And I preferred the emptiness of our condo to seeing anyone else. Plus, we both know I wasn't alone there.

We lived in a condo in a brownstone off Paulina and 18th Street, in Pilsen. The building was one of many properties in the neighborhood being bought by investors and redesigned into condos. Ours was on the first floor, with two units above us and a garden unit below. It was bigger than the apartment we'd rented and barely fit in, but still meant to be our starter home, something we could rent out later on once we bought our own house and adopted a dog or ten.

Three things pissed off Diane right out of the gate: a lot of these remodeled condos were just hiding deal-breaker problems behind the new fixtures and Ikea cabinets; we had wasted our money on a condo instead of buying a house—paying twice as much as a unit was going for when she lived in Pilsen; and you let me put my name on the mortgage too.

She wasn't swayed by all the shops and restaurants opening in Pilsen, the influx of art kids and white kids and microbreweries and food trucks. Even after we showed her the Zillow listing that estimated the value had *increased* since we bought the condo, she still stuck out her chin and shook her head. She barely spoke to us the day your stepdad helped us move, leaning against the breakfast nook and playing Candy Crush on her phone while we chipped the doorframes bringing in the couches. We'd made a dumb move in her mind and that was that. All our evidence to the contrary only proved it was the third thing that bothered her most.

And *that*, neither of us could argue that. I mean you tried. But calling your mom classist and ignorant and a hypocrite didn't sway her. What did she tell you? "I'm not one of your college friends. That shit don't bother me." They left and you said talking with your mom was like talking to the comment thread for some article.

Diane's opinion of me didn't have anything to do with how I treated you, but what she could intuit about me. She prided herself on being able to read people, and what she saw in my eyes and the corners of my mouth, she didn't like. Her salad days in Pilsen had inured her to scumbags and their offspring. Plus she went to high school with my two youngest uncles and saw the crew they ran with, and it wasn't too much of a stretch to think the whole family tree was rotten. Enough for anyone to want their daughter to cut her losses before this facehugger named Thiago clamped his bony legs around her skull and secreted his evil embryos down her throat.

Your mom went to school with my father's brothers. Spin the wheel on that side of the family and any name served as a perfect example of the caliber of DNA being produced. While Pancho Villa was touring the Mexican highlands for reinforcements, my dad's grandfather put together a faction posing as one of his posses and robbed people of their horses and anything else they could sell. His great-grandmother practiced witchcraft and sniffed a rag soaked in gasoline during the pregnancy of all eleven of her kids, nine of whom actually survived.

For the first eleven years of my life, I never knew any of them existed. What I knew about my father came from the handful of times he visited us over the years. A weekend here, a holiday there. My mom said he was a businessman who traveled a lot for his job. Even as a kid, he never struck me as the professional business type. I walked home from school one day and found my mom crying and laughing in the kitchen. "You're father's coming to live with us!" she said, rubbing a bunched paper towel against her nose.

It wasn't until he'd moved in and we went to the parties of his extended family that the cousins my age told me the truth. Their Tío Raul wasn't a businessman. He'd lived in Chicago all his life and drove a school bus for work. Those two other boys giving me hard looks from the corner? They were his "real" sons. All these years, he was living with his "real" family, and everyone knew about me and my mom but no one ever talked about it. Not when Raul scored a big settlement with the City of Chicago after a snowplow T-boned him in an intersection, and he was living large and spreading all the money around to friends and family. Eventually the cash was squandered and he got hooked on pills. His wife kicked him out. That's why he came to live with us. Because he had nowhere else to go. Not even his own brothers offered their homes to him.

My dad told me these things about his family usually slouched over in the driver's seat after picking me up from school, strings of saliva sometimes dribbling down his chin. He would get on these tangents and just drive and drive with me trapped in the passenger seat, bracing before every traffic light. He seemed proud of these crazy stories because he always told them when he was fucked-up, which was often.

They were all like this, brash and out of control. I was the quiet kid, taking after my mom and the passive, isolated way she went through life. She moved to Chicago to be closer to my father, knowing he refused to acknowledge the child she was carrying as his, and her own family disowned her for it. It only made me revert into myself even more, seeing the family tree I was a part of, what I was wrapped into.

Hanging by their necks from our family tree were women who were raped to death, who were raped and then beaten to death by their fathers for being so stupid as to allow themselves to be spoiled.

Somewhere in there was an ancestor who married his sister and birthed another twisted branch off the tree.

There were people in my family who died from bot flies. Drive-bys. Secret lovers.

The herniated roots of the Alvarez family that slithered across the border managed to ensnare other root systems and choke them out for their own absorption. This was mostly done through marriage or getting knocked up.

There were bullet holes in the furniture at my grandmother's house from when my grandfather went crazy and threatened to kill her, firing his .38 into the walls and the sofa and photos around her, daring her to move.

After he moved in with us, my dad took me to visit my uncles who were away at "college." We would wait in a room with other families until the uncle for that visit walked in wearing a brown jumpsuit. I would ask him how college was and he would say good, "Good, mijo."

Sometimes I'd come home from school or the park and my dad would hit me on sight. I would rub the back of my head, chewing on my cheek to keep from crying, and pick up my baseball cap. "What did you do that for?"

Walking toward the kitchen, he'd say, "Ya sabes, güey." *You know why, dumbass.* He was banking on the fact that I was his seed, and I had probably already done something to deserve it.

The fact that I didn't have a record and didn't have any kids by the time I was eighteen labeled me as "the Golden Child" to some in the family, and a wannabe white person to others. I know they all got a little satisfaction out of hearing I dropped out of college to help my mom take care of my dad when first his kidneys crapped out, then his liver. My cousin Linda was the one who got me into working for ride-sharing companies and delivery apps to support us while Raul wasted away in a hospice. "Two years of college just to run to me for help," she said over the phone, when I told her about my first fare. Her laughter through the receiver hurt my ear.

To your mom or anyone else looking at the projection of my life, I was a burnout, someone going nowhere. The first time you took me to meet your parents, I introduced myself as an independent contractor, and Diane asked in what trade.

"Uber, Lyft, and TaskRabbit," I said.

"Apps?" she said, and I could feel your arm squeezing around mine as you smiled through it. Over lunch, me and you did the thing where couples tell a story together by volleying it back and forth between them.

"Remember how I told you I bought all this IKEA furniture?" you asked her. "And it took me *four* hours to put together my desk? Well, there's this app called Task-Rabbit . . ."

"Eh, what's up, Doc?" I said, which usually killed, every other time we told this story. Diane just turned in her seat and looked back to you. Not having that laugh beat tripped you up on your next line.

"Uh, it—it's an app where you can post a job you need done and it'll match you up with someone who can do it for you."

"She needed help with the dresser," I said.

"And the clothes rack."

"And the TV stand."

Diane bunched her lips and nodded, shrugged. I knew that look. It was the same one you gave if we ate a mediocre meal at a restaurant, if we saw a movie I wanted to see and I asked you how you liked it. It meant you had your own thoughts but didn't want to hurt my feelings or get into some argument. Here your mom was, giving both of us the same look. But the ball was rolling on our story, and we stopped caring about her reactions, talking to each other instead, telling ourselves how it happened.

It was your first place after U of C. You were two years older than me. Diane *loved* that.

We went about our work quietly, me working on the TV stand while you unpacked boxes. I still remember the surprised look on your face when you saw the stand was finished and I had already connected the television to your Apple TV box.

"Finished?" you said, coming from the kitchen.

I wanted to make sure the connection was good, so I was scrolling through Sahara Plus looking for a movie to use as a test, but I couldn't just pick any movie. "I don't want to ruin your Suggested Categories."

"It doesn't matter to me," you said.

"Here," I said, and clicked on Cary Fukunaga's *Jane Eyre*. "This is right up your alley."

You shuffled closer to me, both of us standing in front of the television. "What makes you think I'll like this?"

"You've got *Emma*, *The Tudors*, *A Room with a View*, and *Downton Abbey* in your Previously Watched list. I'm guessing you're an Anglophile who's got a thing for period dramas. Ten bucks says there's a tea set in one of those boxes."

A smile crept behind the hand you held up to your lips. "Lucky guess."

We watched the first few minutes standing there in silence. You left and I turned off the television, assuming we were getting back to work, but you only went to grab your phone. "What happened to the movie?"

"Oh. Nothing," I said.

I could smell the soap in your hair when you approached me with your phone, a food delivery app opened. "Hungry?" you said.

"Yeah," I said, pushing my tongue against the roof of my mouth to keep from smiling. "I could eat."

Six months later, I moved into that same apartment. I put my clothes in the dresser I had helped build. I met your parents, met your friends. We fought. We made love. We each quietly hoped the other would grow out of their failings but learned to talk about it when that didn't happen.

We flew to England and visited Highclere Castle. We flew to L.A. and visited the New Beverly Cinema. We made plans. We put things off.

When my mom was diagnosed with cancer three years later, we shared going to the hospital with her for treatment. She died and the funeral home filled with faces I barely recognized, half strangers who felt the need to sit in the first row and tell me all about how they knew her, how they loved her. I assumed they were looking for money, but what they were really after was her death itself, like they were drawn to it and wanted to be part of it, leeching something out of the moment. I could picture them flipping through obituaries, looking for names they recognized, loading up their cars to insert themselves into someone else's grief. And you took me outside and told me you loved me, told me none of them would be invited to our wedding.

"Our wedding?"

"Yeah," you said, and pulled me, by the lapels, closer. "If you feel like you're going to be alone now, you won't. I love you, Branson. You're stuck with me."

After we bought the condo, Olivia and Terrence came over for dinner as our first guests. They would also be the last people we entertained together—another dinner in July, three months before it happened.

Writing that out, it seems long to go without company

over. I guess I could use the AC as an excuse, except a part of me knows it was because I hated having to be "on" around people, and you knew that. So you met people out rather than bring them home, and I got to lie on the couch in shorts and zone out in front of the TV. A real charmer.

At night I would wake up to these loud, hammering noises coming from the front of our place, like a semitruck was being unloaded in our living room. Clanging metal. The noise would reverberate like a scream. The first time, I shot out of bed and ran to the living room, switched on the lights, but everything was how we left it. The sound was gone. I looked out the front windows, but there was nothing.

"You didn't hear that?" I said, getting back into bed.

"What?" you said, turning over, your hair ironed across your face.

"The noise."

"What noise?"

The second time it was you who heard it, shaking me until I opened my eyes and sat up. It sounded like the central air had kicked on and maybe a screw was loose on one of the vents, so the forced air pushing between the slats was banging the frame against the wall. As soon as we got up, the noise stopped. We walked through the condo, checking the hallway, the bathroom, the second bedroom, the kitchen, and the living room, too sleepy to be scared.

My working theory had to do with the AC. The inspector had said in his report that we'd have to replace the blower in three or five years. It was old and as soon as the evaporator pan cracked completely—because he saw it was barely held together with epoxy—we'd have to get a new one. Maybe it had crapped out three years early.

And you complained about cold spots in the condo, different from the air-conditioning. Sometimes you walked into a room and it felt like a polar vortex had found its way inside, but if you walked a little farther into the room the coldness would be gone.

At night the floorboards creaked, and I explained it away as just the floor settling. No big deal. Except you woke me up one night and we listened to the slats of hardwood creak, first in the living room and then in the kitchen, the hallway, the slats groaning as the noise drew closer. Of course nothing was there when I got up to check.

I cleared my schedule on TaskRabbit and switched the Lyft app off to be home for the HVAC tech. Besides refilling the Freon, he couldn't find anything wrong. As he was leaving, the UPS guy showed up with a small box in his hands. Your Itza had arrived.

The next night, that last time Olivia and Terrence showed up for dinner, I took their coats and you showed off our new smart speaker developed by Sahara. It was called Itza. You were so proud of how you had programmed it yourself. A glossy white orb about the size of one of those big wooden knobs at the end of a fancy wooden bed frame. It looked like at any moment it could roll off the mantel but didn't.

Itza functioned like a personal assistant, synced to your phone, with access to all your apps and our shared Sahara account, so we could make purchases, but she could also tell us the balance of our checking accounts, track our caloric intake, and tell us when someone's birthday was a week away.

"Itza," you said, and the orb lit up, alert, a divine white light that patterned its shell like a soccer ball, the light collapsing into one hexagon that signaled the location of your voice. "Play Selena station." The white hexagon pulsed for a few seconds.

"Playing Selena station, now." Her voice was followed by cumbia music blaring through its surround speaker.

I never wanted the thing. My life was already run by apps. I hated having to say her name first before she would do anything. She made me think of HAL from *2001*, down to her dulcet voice.

"Watch," I said, and Olivia and Terrence came up next to me, the three of us standing in front of the Itza. "Itza, open the pod bay doors."

A web of white hexagons spun and collapsed in our direction. "I'm sorry, Dave. I'm afraid I can't do that."

"Itza," Terrence said. "What is the answer to life?"

"Forty-two," she said, in her flat tone that somehow managed to convey eagerness. I pictured a white woman, mid-forties, with two boys and a husband who worked in middle management. She walked to work in tennis shoes and drank a glass of red wine every other day. Housed in this oversize cue ball.

You had made a paella you weren't entirely sure you could pull off, but the four of us destroyed it. Terrence was ripping pieces of bread and cleaning the juice off his plate, it was that good.

You were telling us about the crazy lady on the train home who wouldn't shut up about her dead cat, the economy, the racist police who molested her. She paced up and down the train, talking to no one and everyone at the same time, until she finally sat down next to you.

"Sorry about your cat," you told her.

"Oh, you heard?" she said.

Itza's voice suddenly boomed over the table. Olivia and Terrence flinched and spun around in their chairs, and we all looked at the glowing hexagon pattern.

"I'm sorry," Itza said. "I can't find the answer to the question you asked."

It was so out of nowhere that we burst out laughing. Itza's volume had somehow raised itself to what felt like the highest setting. Maybe the thing had restarted on its own, set itself back to factory settings? The four of us traced your story back, but we couldn't figure out what could have triggered her.

It.

The condo wasn't perfect, but we kept that to ourselves. The last person we could talk to was your mom. It would only affirm her judgments, which meant we couldn't ask your stepdad for help on the AC.

It also meant you couldn't complain to your mom about the unit above us. When she decided to visit unannounced and asked how things were going, you had to swallow your words and say things were great, everything was great.

The neighbors upstairs, the husband worked third shift. His heavy feet would slam down the back stairs, waking one of us up. And if he wasn't enough of a dick, he'd start his car and the headlights would shine into our bedroom, from the carport just outside our windows. We had to go to the store and buy thick late-night-talk-show curtains and get them fitted for our windows. They did the job, except some nights I'd wake up to his steps and hear the car start and see the outline of light around the curtains, so that the window looked like a door, its frame illuminated with light.

More than once it tricked me, in my dream-sleep haze trying to stagger to the bathroom. Instead of going right I'd go left and my hand would rub against the curtains, trying to turn a knob that wasn't there.

It was funny the first couple times, until it wasn't.

One of the last times, I didn't stop turning my hand against the curtain until the cloth sound woke you up, and you grabbed me by the shoulders and whispered my name. "Thiago, Thiago, wake up."

"What?" I tried clinging to the bits of dream you woke

me out of. Something about water. I remembered waves, standing on the edge of land, like a cliff. I was supposed to do something, but I couldn't remember what.

Two balls of white light blazed into our bedroom when I opened the curtains and pulled up the blinds, shining around the pillars and stairs connected to our decks. The truck's engine idled.

I threw my hands up like what the fuck. If he saw me, if he said something or gave me the finger, the headlights washed it away.

"Thiago," you said again.

This miserable fucking couple thought they could make everyone else's life a living hell. It was some twisted way of them getting power, you said. What they couldn't deal with themselves, they took out on other people. She screamed at the garbage truck guys for putting the cans so far away. He let their cat piss and shit in the downstairs neighbors' herb garden. If the mail lady accidentally put our mail in their slot, they automatically shredded it.

"I didn't know that was yours," she said, holding the door open just enough for you to see her face.

"Our name is on our mail slot," you said.

She sucked her teeth. "Then talk to the mail lady. Maybe she can't read." And she slammed her door shut. They loved slamming doors.

"Thiago . . ."

"This fucking guy." I lowered the blinds and went for my shoes.

"Thiago, wait."

Your head was turned to the side like you were listening for something. I stayed still. The only sound I heard was the guy's car reversing out of the carport and into the alley. I was about to say we should go to bed but stopped. Both of us jumped back from the window.

To the right of the window frame, something was scratching the inside of the wall. It stopped and scratched again but in a different spot, closer to the corner and a few feet higher, without us hearing the rat or squirrel or whatever it was climb the studs it would take to get there.

An animal, that's what we told ourselves. Except the pest control guy wasn't so sure. Vermin in the walls sounded more like a patter, their tiny feet running up and down the frame. If what we heard sounded like scratching against the drywall, it could be a cat. He asked if the other tenants had pets.

We didn't know. "But the scratching moved," I said. "From the top of the frame all the way down to the corner there, in less than a few seconds."

"Could be more than one, or squirrels. Or maybe it's a rat that's trapped and trying to gnaw its way through."

He drilled a hole and fed a long cable into the wall. Attached to the other end of the cable was what looked like a drill with a monitor on it. It was called a borescope, and the cable was an optic device he could maneuver to find any evidence of something in our walls. He

spent over an hour looking before he drilled a hole in another spot, fed the cable through there and looked some
more. He didn't find any nests, any droppings, any runs of
food left by a critter. It was clean. He checked the interior
parts of the wall where we heard the scratching, and there
were no marks, no shavings anywhere.

You had walked into the condo holding a package. "Did
you buy something online?"

"No," I said. "Did you?"

I dried my hands and leaned over the breakfast bar to
see you tear the flaps open, pull out a line of pillow-shaped
bubble wrap.

"What is it? I can't see."

You pulled out a floppy pink dildo. The box fell. We
both just stared at it wiggling in your hand before it settled into a lazy lean over your wrist.

We checked the shipping label and the address was
right, addressed to *me*, but charged on a credit card you
used strictly for groceries and restaurants because the
points tripled. Connected to our Sahara Prime account,
sure, but not the designated card that would get automatically pulled for a purchase.

I logged into my account to print out the return label,
but the option wasn't there. I emailed customer service and
they emailed back within the day. Turns out, for products

that might get soiled by the human body—like the cuff on a heart rate monitor, underwear, dildos—Sahara will just refund the money, no return necessary.

The dildo was already feeling like that one drunk friend who wasn't getting the hint to just go home. I tossed it in a paper bag, then a black garbage bag, then poured the used coffee grounds out of our coffee maker over it, just to prevent any rat or raccoon from digging through the trash and scurrying down our alley with a rubber cock in its mouth. You thought it was funny enough, watching me drop the bag in someone else's dumpster.

"You're acting like you used it," you said.

"Just making sure you don't go back for it when I go to work."

In the middle of the night I'd wake up to roll into a new position, and before falling asleep again, I'd hear a voice in the hallway, the faint glow of Itza's holy light spread on the wall outside our door. Itza coming to life and greeting someone, "Hello."

I was never conscious enough to get out of bed, just awake enough to register it. A blurry film over my eyes, so when I turned to you, you looked like you were underwater.

Sometimes it sounded like, "Hello?"

———

I still pull your hair out of my shirts. I'll throw one on and feel a crease against my skin. A single strand is enough to make me wiggle around, reach through my collar and down the back for something I can't place but know is there. Reaching for something ethereal until it glides between my fingers and I pull it out and suspended in the air is a dark strand of your hair, light flaring off the curls.

We kept getting packages. All of them addressed to me.

The box tape gave it away, Sahara's logo running from top to bottom, spliced with an announcement for the new Itza. I took the box inside and opened it. It was thinner than the box with the dildo, the size of a tablet, maybe an e-reader I wouldn't be too eager to return. It had a flap along the edge that pulled the top half of the box off, and I sighed when I saw it was a book. Easy return.

The cover was all black with red lettering, an odd font and ultra-glossy. The author's name had too many vowels for me to even try to pronounce. The title: *How to Contact the Dead.*

It's easy to see now how we should have nipped it in the bud sooner. We should have deleted our Sahara Plus account, unplugged Itza, moved. But we had monthly order subscriptions tied to our account, and as long as those return labels printed without pushback, I was willing to put up with it to avoid having to go to the store. We returned the twelve bottles of ipecac you got at work and the samurai sword we found leaning against our door. We performed mental gymnastics trying to recall something either of us said around Itza that could have been construed as an order for a hundred mousetraps. We deleted every shipping address except our home, deleted every credit card except one, unplugged Itza unless we wanted to hear music. Two days later another box was sitting outside our door.

"What is it?" you said, and I turned the container around so you could read the label: *Industrial Strength Lye*.

I printed out two return labels, one for the lye, and one for Itza. This was after I opened a customer service tab and chatted with a rep who said the best they could do for us was replace this faulty model with a new one.

The last package we ever got was that new Itza. The dildo became a story I shelled out at parties when it was my turn to talk. From our bedroom you'd call for her to tell you the weather, and she'd respond. Music played when we wanted it. Instead of googling something to settle a stupid argument, we asked her. It. The soft chime of Itza's alarm in the mornings. I'd wake up to your back and slide to your side, nuzzling your hair until it was out of my face. Not able to see your face but knowing you were smiling.

In the movies, if every guy in an indie romance wanted a manic pixie dream girl, then you were my Sarah Connor girl. Strong jawed, road rager, hell-bent on achieving your goals, who also believed people could be good if you were patient with them: "Come with me if you want to live and let live."

The way this would have worked in the movies, you would have been the first to sense something was wrong. You would have told me about this weird feeling you were having and I would have dismissed it. But you didn't see it coming. No funny feeling or women's intuition. No foreboding sense of something on the horizon. You were just as unassuming as I was.

In the movies, that's why you died first. Because you were too smart for your own good. You'd figured it out before the film's run time, so you had to go. In the movies, you would be my inciting incident, as if I was the more interesting one to follow, like I had more to offer. In what universe was that true? Not this one. Sarah Connor was always a main character, at least in the ones that were any good.

It was late, a few hours after we went to bed, and I woke up standing in front of the window with my hand pushing into the curtains, trying to open a door framed in light. The rest of the room was dark, but I could make out the shape of you under the comforter.

I staggered to the bathroom, felt for the seat to lift, because as long as I didn't turn on the light, I could convince myself I was still sleeping and fall back into it as soon as I laid down.

Midstream, light stretched across the hall.

"Hit it," Itza said, and an acoustic guitar strummed a country tune, something like a tambourine accompanying it.

The panic shot into my brain all at once. The song played and echoed through the living room and kitchen. I felt the wall as I made my way to the front of our place.

"You may think I don't hear you, and that might make you blue . . ."

The white orb was pulsing, its hexagons glowing and then spinning. Its light spread across the floor, spilling onto the leather couch, reaching across the walls, the quartz countertop. My feet painted in its haze, and the hardwood looking oily in the glare.

"Itza," I said, "off."

It couldn't locate my voice and kept spinning.

"But I've got plenty of time, so who you talkin' to . . . ?"

"Itza, off."

"Our connection, you can't deny . . ."

Something in her voice cracked, the audio version of a screen scrambling. A chord in the automated bundle that made up her voice had split, and for the first time I noticed how heavy I was breathing. The parts of my skin exposed to the white glow prickled, and I could feel myself bracing for something, though I couldn't tell you what.

"To give you these gifts, makes me high . . ."

I looked down at my feet. The oily reflection running across the slats had poured over them, rooting me into the hardwood. I couldn't move because I was too busy focusing on squeezing every muscle in my body, holding myself together. The molars in the back of my mouth hummed. I had this gunmetal fact running through me—if I stopped tensing up I would scatter into dust.

"Itza . . ." And now it was my voice that was chipping away, the words hissed out, an unknown weight compressing my breath.

Her words trudged through an atmospheric mud, warping the song into something not her voice, not human.

"I'm here whether you need me, here whether you see me, and that ain't bad . . ."

A shadow passed in my peripheral.

"I'm here whether you need me, here whether you see me, so don't be sad . . ."

You reached behind the table and unplugged her. It. I snapped out of it, jumping back so hard I slammed against the wall. My ears were filled with mothballs, the whole room buzzing with something.

"The hell is going on?" you said. I didn't know how to answer that.

When we told people what was happening, the conversations usually started with stories about glitches and led to surveillance. Everyone had their own story about Itza piping up on her own. Maribel was sitting there alone, reading, and out of nowhere Itza started in on a knock-knock joke. Oscar, who went all-in with the deluxe model and two mini versions, said his whole family was asleep when the power went out. Sometime in the night the power kicked back on, and all three Itzas rebooted at once, calling into the house, "HELLO! HELLO! HELLO!"

Mysterious purchases? Happened to your friend's mom. At a happy hour thing your job was having, she told us how she had to go over and help her mom figure out how to return a fifteen-foot trampoline.

That creepy song? Congratulations, it's an Easter egg feature. Terrance heard it when he asked Itza to play some country music.

"Yeah, but . . ." you said, and just let it go, letting your friends assure us it was the speaker, that we just had to lower the volume, maybe move it away from the TV. We'd share a glance and shrug, thinking the same thing. *It's not the same.*

No one ever suggested a priest. Or a medium.

We were both dancing around what we really wanted to say. It wasn't just Itza and the song and the purchases, but the banging noises, the cold spots, the scratching in the wall. That window. The one I kept waking up trying to open. One day I parked in the carport and saw four dead birds on the ground below it. Blood and grease smeared against the glass where they'd smashed their heads.

The creepy coincidences, the weird stuff, was building, gathering into itself. As long as we didn't give it a name, it stayed amorphous. It couldn't take shape.

Calling the real estate agent was your idea. Not our agent, but the seller's. We kind of knew who the seller was, but getting in contact with him was impossible. Our brownstone was one of a handful of properties this guy owned in Pilsen, and it was easy to spot his buildings because the exteriors were all painted the same beige color, with black trim and black vinyl window frames. The other properties housed businesses and were run by building managers who weren't about to offer up his name and direct phone number. The guy didn't show up for our closing, so even if we knew his name, we wouldn't know his face.

We kept the paperwork from the closing in an empty Ugg shoebox under our bed, and sitting cross-legged on the bedroom carpet, papers forming concentric circles around you, you found the real estate agent's name and agency.

Still, I didn't think he would help. If we wanted to bitch about the property, he was probably going to tell us to talk to the inspector, not him.

"Then let him tell us no. We're the ones stuck here, Thiago. We have to at least try."

You put the phone on speaker and set it on the counter, and we both listened to it ring. He picked up and you introduced yourself, giving him our address and telling him we met at the condo closing. He sounded apprehensive. You asked if he could tell us anything about the history of the building before it was rehabbed. Did something happen here? Was there anything weird about the space?

We stared at the phone, waiting for him to say something.

"Why do you ask?" he finally said.

The cold spots you had been walking through, it felt like one of them had passed through me as we stood there. My internal organs felt jumbled into the wrong spots.

"Because we've been experiencing things," you said, the mix of fear and adrenaline making the whites of your eyes pop. "I know this sounds crazy. It's just—"

"I'm sorry, ma'am, but any problems with appliances should have been brought up at the closing."

"No, you're not hearing me."

His voice got faraway, like he was shifting the phone off his shoulder to end the call. "Please refer to the contract."

You asked if that was the same contract requiring the seller to disclose any defects with the property to the buyer. Like our water pipe leaking into the unit below us, and how the downstairs neighbors told us they had repeatedly asked the agent's client to fix it, but he never did, and maybe the agent didn't know about this preexisting problem, but maybe he did.

"Excuse me—"

But you blurted something about fiduciary responsibility and small claims court, and that shut him up. We both looked at each other. Next thing he said was, "Hold on a sec."

The sound of wind cutting across the receiver suddenly disappeared, followed by a sharp thump. "Sorry, just getting into my car." He took a deep breath. "Look, I can reach out to Mr. Groff and see if he knows anything, but I don't think he'll be much help. He isn't much of a hands-on guy when it comes to tenants. But I toured the building with him after the last unit cleared. The unit you purchased. An elderly woman had been living there for ages, no one knew quite how long. She was . . . very upset about being forced to move. I don't know whether she did this in retaliation or if this was how she was living, but the unit was filthy. There was garbage piled in the corners, the toilet and tub were backed up. The smell was intolerable."

The line went quiet. We looked at each other again. "Hello?" you said. "Did we lose you?"

"In the living room was a circle of melted candles. In the center of it was . . . an animal carcass. You don't realize how hard it is to identify an animal without fur. Or skin."

Your hands flew up to your mouth. "Oh my God."

The agent kept talking. He said on the wall facing the carcass was a large rectangular shape drawn in blood.

"What do you mean?"

"Looked like a giant door," he said. "I don't know. I told Mr. Groff to call the police. This was obviously animal cruelty, but I think he just hired a couple guys to come in and clean it all up before the demo started . . . Are you still there?"

Something in the living room caught my eye. A flash of movement. We both looked up and you extended your arm across my chest like we were about to rear-end a car.

A wave of white light slid across Itza's surface. The hexagons glowed and then spun around, trying to locate our voices. Was she listening to us, or had she been listening to us? It didn't matter. The hexagons spun another rotation and vanished. Whatever it was, it was too late to do anything about it.

Every night before bed, I set the alarm. That was my thing, set the alarm. It just happened, the way you always washed the clothes, and I folded them. I ran the dishwasher, you emptied it.

You never asked me to plug Itza back in after the whole song incident. I just did it. I had gotten used to calling it out: "Itza, set the alarm for 6:00 a.m." I could have just as easily set it on my phone. That's the cruelest part, that your life came down to me preferring Itza's soft chime over anything on my phone.

I know, if you could, you'd say it wasn't my fault. You were thoughtful like that.

The following morning, six o'clock came and went. The alarm never went off. The room was usually pitch-black when we woke up, not indigo, and you sprang out of bed, throwing the comforter off and muttering, "Oh shit oh shit oh shit oh shit," still half asleep. I woke up to the shower hiss.

"Itza, time check," you called out. I staggered into the living room in my boxers and stared at Itza like she would explain herself, apologize. But the milky orb remained blank, its dead stare pointed back at me.

I went to make coffee and you were already running out of the bathroom to the bedroom, your hair tied in a bun even though it was still wet.

"Fuck fuck fuck fuck fuck . . ."

"Don't worry," I said. "I'll drive you."

"Too much traffic," you said, hopping out of the bedroom into the hall, already in a skirt and blazer, struggling with your heels.

"Seriously, I can take you."

"Okay I gotta go bye—"

You kissed me. I smelled the conditioner in your hair.

The door closed behind you. I took the French press off the stove and poured the coffee into my thermos, resigned to starting my day earlier than I planned.

"Itza," I said. "What's your fucking problem?"

The white hexagons spun. "Okay, well I'll be here when you need me."

You'd say it wasn't the kid's fault either. He was just on that platform looking for an easy mark. You would have pointed to his clean record, how his dad was killed by a drunk driver, how at fourteen he had to find his family an apartment they could afford, translating for his mom the leasing terms of the thirty-something white dude slumlord who owned practically the whole block, buying foreclosed places and only advertising in church bulletins and Spanish flyers. You would have seen how the first time this kid walked home from school the gangbangers asked where he was from, and not understanding the question, he said "Jalisco," and got stomped then and there. How a warring group of gangbangers saw him fumbling with his keys later, bloody and bug-eyed, and said they could protect him, but he had to pass a few initiation tests first.

I was driving a passenger to the airport when I got the call.

"This is Officer Collins . . ." she said.

My heart jumped a gear. The traffic outside the windshield seemed to grow closer and farther at the same time. "Okay?"

"Is this Thiago Alvarez? Is your wife Vera Alvarez?"

"Is everything okay?"

"Are you driving, Mr. Alvarez? Can you pull over?"

The phone felt like an ice block numbing my fingers and flowing through the rest of me, my ear going cold, the ice block's whisper unspooling into my ear as she talked, into the black space behind my dull eyes, staring out through the windshield, a crossing guard signaling for me to drive through now, sir, *sir*, and then muffled thumps on my driver's-side window, my passenger jumping out of the car, freaked out.

After Officer Collins finished talking, I asked if you were okay. She said the EMTs told her that as soon as she got a hold of the spouse, to tell him to get to the hospital as soon as possible.

My next call was to your mom. I told her what had happened, swinging a U-turn across both flows of traffic, horns blaring around me. She kept screaming into the phone, a sound that's carved into my bones like grooves in a vinyl record.

"The assailant was absconding with a commuter's phone when he made contact with the victim at the top of the platform steps. The victim was rendered unsecure in her footing and fell backwards . . ."

Police report talk.

Not a *piece of shit*, but the *assailant*.

Not my *wife*, but the *victim*.

The first phase of his initiation was to steal something the gang could sell. Just as the L was coming into the station, he ripped an iPhone out of some woman's hand, her headphones going with it, and as he fled to the stairs something caught his attention and he looked back.

He never explained why he looked back. Maybe to see if the woman was chasing him? In the police report he said he heard someone call his name. The prosecutor would press him on this at the trial, and his neck veins would throb like every muscle in his body was tense, but he'd shake his head, refusing to answer. Even his public defender couldn't get him to explain why.

So for some mysterious reason he looked back, and this made him bump into another woman waiting for the train, causing him to spin around, and you were probably running up the stairs because you must have heard the screech of the train arriving into the station, and you were running dead center up the stairwell because the lady holding the banister was too slow, and the kid righted himself and kept sprinting and barreled into you, and I want to believe you never saw him, that you had your head down, because I don't want to think his face was the last face you ever saw, that his eyes were the last you ever locked with, and it's easier to think this because you fell so fully, not grasping on to anything, no tangling with this kid to bring him down with you. You fell like you were standing with your back to an in-ground pool and someone pushed you in.

Police interviewed the old woman on the stairs who saw you fall. They wanted the play-by-play and she kept going on about the sound of your head hitting the concrete floor.

Comas are hard to predict, which made the doctors nervous when it came to explaining things to me and your mom. All outcomes fell hard onto the worst possible scenario.

I once read a book by a Holocaust survivor who said those who were crushingly optimistic were the ones to die first. Not killed, but died, either from illness or organ failure or straight-up fatigue. I think doctors take that approach with delivering news. Instead of dressing up your chances of recovery, they talked about the percentage of coma patients who never wake up again.

In the hospital bed you looked sick, flushed, but not unconscious. I understood the doctor when he said you probably couldn't hear us, and I understood the uncomfortable expression on his face when I kept saying your name.

"It doesn't hurt to talk if you want," he said. "We've had patients physically react to the sound of someone's voice, a song, but these are extremely rare cases, oftentimes revolving around comas that result from a bacterial infection, not trauma. We don't know what will get through to her, what she can hear or feel. So it isn't in vain to try."

Nurses visited the room and flexed your limbs, because the hours and days in bed were crushing you. Your body would start to curl into itself, like some invisible force crumpling you into a paper ball. And any recovery, like you waking up out of the coma, meant a life warped by the effects commonly associated with traumatic brain injuries.

I researched the cost of at-home care, live-in nurses. Watched videos of spouses sitting next to their husband or wife who had survived a car crash or work accident. "You take it one day at a time," a wife said, her husband wearing an Iron Man shirt, looking up at the ceiling with his mouth open, eyes unfocused, who grunted in what must have been pleasure, because the corners of his mouth curled into a smile. His wife turned to him and put her hand into his, trying to talk to him as he kept emitting echoey sounds from his throat, like boats approaching in a fog.

No one stopped the kid when he bumped into you and you opened your head on the landing. He squirmed between the growing crowd and got away. But the police managed to get a good look at his face on the security cameras.

Since it dealt with public transit, local news kept up with the story, but no one ever tried to sensationalize it. Until the cops arrested the kid and it turned out he didn't have any papers.

I could picture you rolling your eyes.

Of course he didn't have papers. Now you'd be the poster girl for the people who blamed everything on immigrants. Your face on white nationalist websites. Life is life.

It being an election year, the candidates and pundits jumped on it. Newspapers fanned the flames and the talk radio hosts and political commentators sank their talons into the story. This was about Immigration. This was about

Urban Crime. This was about Violence Against Women, Race, Justice.

You were a foregone conclusion. Your story stood in for a bigger idea, an agenda that had been raging since before we were born. We were caught in its teeth now.

At least the cameramen outside the hospital were cool. They gave me a wide berth when I walked from the lobby to my car. Your mom got a lawyer, and through him put out a statement asking for privacy.

Certain activists with high profiles called to discuss a hospital visit, possibly address the press on our behalf. Presidential candidates, celebrities attached to human rights groups. I told them to fuck off, and that was the tame option compared to Diane's response.

Your mom and stepdad stayed during the day, mostly your mom. After work I'd go over and she would step out to shower at home, change. We switched nights sleeping over. It'd be too late at night to notice, but in the mornings I could see the change in your face, cheekbones that were more severe than the day before, your fingertips yellowing. Friends stopped by once in a while and after we exchanged pleasantries, their eyes inevitably fell on you, and they'd ask about your progress, like there was ever any progress, and I'd give the latest seizure number you were up to and they'd say you were tough. You were a fighter.

You weren't ready to give up. All the stuff you'd say about a premature baby.

Your stepdad showed up to the hospital and looked flustered. I told him I was going home to catch a few hours and he barely mustered a grunt. I caught an elevator before it closed and Diane was already inside it, like she hadn't gotten out when it opened the first time.

She had freckles now, busted blood vessels around her eyes, tissues stuffed into her sleeves. She looked at me and I wanted to take it all away, just for her sake.

"Give her to me," she said. "We actually own our home. We can put in the ramp and lift and whatever else she needs. I can give her the care she needs, Thiago. I'll retire. What are you going to do?"

Even before this, I had a dream that I showed up to the hospital and walked into your room and you were awake. Your jaw hung loose and a fat pale tongue writhed in the air, and you made distasteful moans, your eyes unable to focus on anything, like nothing was there, your hands curled against your wrists and waving them around. Skin like wax. The front of your gown soaked in saliva. Your mom sat on the bed with you and looked up, beaming.

"My baby's back," she said.

I got home and rolled into bed, but my brain kept racing through scenarios and all the things that still needed to get done. I had to call the insurance company again because a ventilator that was quoted as being eligible for our insurance wasn't being covered by the insurance. Your boss wanted to know if he should put you on a sabbatical or just use the banked sick and vacation time you had accrued. "Which would she prefer?" he said.

I scrolled through my phone before finally deciding to get out of bed, the afterglow of the screen still in my eyes. I headed into the kitchen and turned on the light. The cupboard was empty of clean cups. I rinsed a coffee mug out of the sink, pushed it against the water dispenser on the fridge door.

Covering the fridge were photos, cards, reminders we had left for each other. All of them held up by tiny magnets, little white rectangles covered with single words in black.

There was a Save the Date, your yoga class schedule, a ten-dollars-off coupon for Benny's, our favorite pizza spot. Right over the water dispenser was the strip of photo booth pictures we took at some work event of yours. Holding it in place in the right-hand corner was a magnet with only two letters: *ha*.

Here you were again. It was like we were having a conversation. I could hear your laugh. Did you mean to do that? How many times had I passed and not noticed? My eyes scanned the fridge for more messages.

A draft swept through the kitchen, windless, but with a severe change in temperature that atomized my skin, the hair on my forearms drying out into quills.

What had finally gotten me out of bed that morning was the constant notifications on my phone, which was sitting in the kitchen, and all the things I still had to do.

I had to figure out how to deactivate my social media accounts because complete strangers were telling me either how sorry they felt or how angry they would be if it was their wife, and what the country should do about illegals, or how I shouldn't blame an underrepresented population for a freak accident.

The hospital diapers were giving you a rash. I needed to buy a different brand.

The assistant state's attorney assigned to your case needed to sit down with me, and as patient as he had been, he didn't want to have to subpoena me to finally show up for court.

I got a message from some guy in Virginia who claimed he had proof you were fake news.

On the fridge, holding up the top corners of the Christmas card your best friend sent us, the magnets read *ha* and *haha*.

My eyes glanced over the yoga schedule and instead of words, instead of the magnets we would use to leave funny sentences for each other, pinned on each corner was *hahaha*, *ha*, *haha*, *ha*. The top right of the fridge where we left the unused words was a cluster of *hahahahahahahaha*.

I stepped back and my coffee mug smashed on the tile at my feet. The entire fridge was covered in laughter.

I looked away from the fridge the way a child turns from the TV when something scary pops up, when all that actually does is give the monster enough time to crawl out of the screen and stand two inches in front of the kid's face for when they turn back. I willed myself to look again and the magnets were just a jumbled soup of words again. The word *love* was holding up our photo booth strip, *fat* and *face* in the top corners of your yoga schedule.

Itza let out a two-toned error sound, and the living room disco-balled with her light. "Hmm, I'm not sure I know what you're looking for," she said.

You weren't awake, but what you were didn't qualify as asleep either. Your eyes were closed and you kept fidgeting, spasming, but I couldn't get you to wake, to tell you it was a bad dream you were having. I stared at the shape of your body under the blanket, the broomstick legs that belonged to an elderly woman, because no way could they be yours. Like some magic trick. It was someone else's body on that bed and you were crouched underneath, your head pushed through a hole below the pillow.

I was in your room, flipping through channels when the remote stopped working and got stuck on a car commercial. I checked the cord connecting the remote to the bed to see if maybe you were lying on it, pinching it. The commercial break ended and *The Exorcist* came on.

The volume didn't come from the television but from a speaker on your bed, so the audio and visuals were disconnected. I was seeing it in front of me but hearing it behind me.

No matter what I pressed, off, power, nothing changed.

It was regular cable so they probably hadn't shown the crucifix masturbation/your-mother-sucks-dicks-in-hell exchange. When we joined the movie, both priests were fatigued and struggling to continue.

I couldn't lower the volume or page the nurse.

Their mouths blew out small clouds of fog. "Why her?" the younger priest said. "Why this girl?"

His voice sent a tremor through my body, and the tremor locked my body into the chair, facing the screen. I felt like I was floating up to the TV, caught in a beam.

"I think the point is to make us despair," the older priest said. "To see ourselves as," he wheezed, "animal and ugly. To make us reject the possibility that God could love us."

If I had to pick a time in all of this, where I thought maybe you were communicating to me, it was that moment in the hospital room.

You were on your way, and somehow you could see what was on the horizon for me, or maybe you could see who was behind it all, and that they were going to stay with me, and maybe you couldn't do anything about it, but before you went wherever you went, you wanted to tell me something, something to take with me into the future. This theory came way later, many deaths later. Too late.

Out in the hall I heard footsteps. A blur of images rushed on the screen, too fast for me to absorb. A nurse knocked at the doorway and leaned in.

"Okay, who's got the lead thumb in here?"

I wasn't there the day it happened. I'm sorry. Your mom called and I stopped getting dressed. She wasn't screaming this time. Her voice was shot from too much of it already. She simply said you were gone. A bad seizure. The doctors couldn't stabilize you.

It's like being at a party and the one friend you know is suddenly gone.

In this world we struggle and bitch and fail and hurt and then weep over someone checking out of it all.

At the funeral your boss collapsed into my arms. "I just want to know," he said, sobbing into my neck. "I just want a sign or something. That she's okay."

That's how I knew to disregard that feeling. If he wanted it, then it wasn't anything special. If friends of friends could go out and get small tattoos in remembrance of you, then it wasn't anything special. The more I tried to get at what

was vital about you, what I could hold on to and say, *This is
still you*, the more I felt like I was grabbing at the tiny black
spots that pop in and out of existence after a hard sneeze.

That first full day alone in our condo, I felt the gulf. How
much had been scooped out of my life. I thought I knew
what grief was when my mother died. But as much as I
loved her, I also wanted her to be free of her suffering. The
fourteen months of cancer treatment allowed me to antic-
ipate her death. She lived her life. You still had so much
ahead of you.

While I was laid up on the couch, my phone vibrated
with a new job. Someone needed a dog walker on short
notice. I called the person back to apologize, to say I must
have left the app on by accident, except when I heard my
voice I realized I had quit instead. As if this person was my
boss.

It was your idea to pay into such a big insurance policy.
To supplement whatever we got from a pension or 401(k).
For when we got old, eventually retired.

Diane had the hospital staff wait for me to get there before they wheeled your body away. After I sat and watched
them zip the bag over your face, after the news channels
confirmed to the public that you had indeed died, after the
funeral came and went, a letter in the mail arrived from
the insurance adviser who sold us the policy. A couple sig-
natures, a copy of your death certificate, and six digits ap-

peared in our bank account, more money than I knew what to do with.

I was ashamed. I thought people could see the money in my facial expressions, that it made me transparent. My life was becoming the second act to a *Dateline* special. Wife dies, husband gets rich.

"It's yours," Diane said. "She would have wanted you to have it."

I wasn't sure what it was you'd have wanted anymore.

You've freed me from being a salary slave, from working as an "independent contractor" for the rest of my life. Diane said I should go back to school. Maybe I could finally do what I've only ever shared with you. The thought of making my own movie scared the hell out of me, but I secretly envied the people who managed to pay their rent working as a film critic.

"You should start a blog," you had said. "Then we can write off going to the movies on our taxes."

But I was full of excuses. Still am. Dropping out of college to help care for my dad was sort of a blessing because I had no idea what I wanted to do for a degree, let alone with my life. I come from a long line of odd-jobbers, natural-born fuckups. Bad hombres. None of them ever worried about their future. Honestly, the only retirement option I might have ever considered was sold by the caliber. You broke that cycle for me. Thank you for that. Second to I love you, that's the thing I keep wanting to say. Thank you. Besides I'm sorry.

———

I'm supposed to move on, get over it, let go. But it's like having an arm amputated and complaining that you can still feel the phantom hand balled into a fist, and it hurts, and they all stare at me like monks in their Zen gardens, and say, "You have to let go." To them, it's a storm you weather, and if I just keep pushing through, I'll come out the other side to a brighter day. A new day. Images of renewal and rebirth. Plant something and watch it grow. Except it doesn't feel that way. No journey, no thing to endure. It feels like a corruption of genes. A double helix scrambled in a petri dish. A puppet forced to work on crossed strings. Those trees that manage to grow around power lines and stay mangled forever.

Some of your friends pointed out my ring, that I still wear it. It never occurred to me not to. The running opinion was that it didn't allow me the chance to move forward. What if I met someone? Wouldn't I feel worse taking off the ring then? They seemed to put a lot of thought into this.

Your mom said these "friends" just wanted to fuck me.

I get now why old cultures and native tribes kept rituals for death. You exorcised the grief with a ritual and it gave everyone something to do, a space to be sad, and after the bereaved lifted that boulder or pierced their scrotum or sipped that hallucinogenic tea, we could all agree

that the dead had been sufficiently mourned. They were
adequately remembered, and none of us would feel guilty
for what felt like a lack of action on our part.

Instead of feeling whatever this was.

I feel it every day. Every day.

What the real estate agent told us was, if we weren't re-
ceiving any of the previous tenant's mail, then she probably filed a change of address with the post office to get
her mail forwarded to her new place. The only thing we
had was a piece of junk mail from a cable company addressed to Fidelia Marroquín or current resident. So what
we could do was mail an envelope first class to Fidelia with
our current address. Under the return address part of the
envelope, we'd write RETURN SERVICE REQUESTED. If the
post office had her new address on file, they would mail
us a notification of the new address. You rubbed your
arms to get rid of the goose bumps inherent with finding
out this stalker loophole existed, but we had to get over it.

We mulled over whether to include some kind of letter
in the envelope, telling her who we were and what was going on, but maybe her knowing more about us wasn't the
best thing to do. I went to the post office and mailed the
first class envelope and forgot about it. Your fall, the hospital visits, your death, pushed it out of my mind. It wasn't

until I checked the mail one day and found a card from the post office with Fidelia Marroquín's new address, a basement unit only five blocks away, that I remembered why we were even looking.

We had been planning on what, telling her to make the cold spots and sounds in the walls go away? Who cared, now that the worst possible thing I could ever imagine had already happened. What was worse than burying you, living in a world where I couldn't see you, where I was locked in this basement existence? There was nothing I wanted to know anymore, except whether killing myself would bring me to you.

I was too afraid to look at my phone and see some think piece about your death being a symbol for anti-globalism, or a call for better social programs. I wanted to choke immigrants and racists alike.

Death to agendas, to the broader picture, the higher purpose. Reporters called my phone and smoke moved through my veins, expelling out of my nostrils.

I didn't want to join some support group, surrounded by knowing glances and sensing without saying the thing that was eating all of us. I didn't want to light a candle, or release a balloon. To do one thing to mean another thing. My wife, the only person I'd choose to sit in a car with in heavy traffic, was dead. And I didn't want to synthesize it into something else. I just wanted to stay with the solid thing, your absence, which in its ethereal quality was more real than the other stuff.

The kid's name was Esteban Lopez, and his face was everywhere, chin pointed out slightly so his neck looked bigger in the mug shot than it actually was. He looked mean, dangerous. Your photo was there too, you at the Metra post in the Loop, the one that reminded you of Paris, arm around it, *Singin' in the Rain* style.

The presidential candidates tweeted out their condolences, practically forced to as right-wing blogs took up the story as proof of the necessity of their own agendas. Some college group did a little digging and found out the last time I voted for anything was eight years ago. They wanted to film my journey as I went to the DMV and renewed my voter registration.

Even the simplest Google search proved there were other photos of Esteban Lopez the media could have used. Ones where he was standing over a birthday cake and his neck was as wide as a shower curtain rod. In that booking photo, if anyone bothered to look—get past the flexed jaw and mottled cheeks and crooked nose—his eyes were round and watery. The CGI eyes they'd put on the animal sidekick in a Pixar movie, not a bad guy.

On some level I knew he didn't intend to run into you. And if there's a God, I hope he forgave him. Because the rest of me was stoking a fire at the core of my being. A subterranean room where the walls dripped orange globs of magma, and I pulled a blade out of a hearth fueled by my hate, forging it with every day I had to see Esteban's face in the news, on my feed, anywhere.

The aunt who gave us the basket of tomatoes, Tía Cheeky, called to see how I was doing, did I need anything, and hey, she heard about the insurance policy, and there was this gastric bypass surgery she was thinking about getting but did I know how pricey it could be, and had I been to the cemetery, because she went every day, still unable to get over your death. Did I know she babysat you as a child, and that you two had a special bond? I could picture the phone cord coiled around her hand, the army of porcelain figurines she kept on top of the television staring back at her.

What I couldn't get over was that you were alone at that train stop. People were there to scream and call 9-1-1, but I wasn't there. And I should have been. I should have driven you to work. You were late. You were late and I could have driven you and you would be alive and I wouldn't have to prop your pillow against my back at night so it could feel like you were lying against me. It wasn't the cemetery I felt I needed to visit, but the train stop.

It was less than two blocks from our house. I put on clothes, pulled another strand of your hair from my collar, and headed out. I'd stopped keeping track of the days at this point, but the atmosphere itself let me know it was the end of a workday, a fatigue in the darkness that settled between the streetlights and dirty headlights of traffic.

I felt like I was walking in your steps, following the last trail you left on this world.

I crossed Paulina and continued down 18th.

A stream of high school kids exited the station. College kids, hipsters, people coming home from work. On their phones or listening to music or talking to friends. From the lobby I could see the steps and all the people walking down them like you were never there, like your body wasn't still there on that ground. Along the wall, where it curved and climbed up toward the platform, there were bouquets of flowers, a crucifix, and even that pissed me off.

Taped over a movie advertisement was a flyer that read *Don't Let Vera Alvarez Die in Vain. Vote for Protecting Americans This November.*

A journalist had contacted me about the proceeds to an online fundraiser. I didn't know what she was talking about. She sent me the link. Someone had set up a Go-FundMe account in your name.

A pink-haired girl on Etsy was selling shirts of a tweet you once wrote: *Fuck demonizing immigrants.*

It was the millennial version of those cultures that exhumed a dead person's corpse and paraded it through the streets, dressing it in new outfits, posing with it for photos.

I wanted to forge something big enough to kill the whole world.

I used your Ventra pass to go through the turnstile. More people walked around me as I climbed the stairs, the chatter of meaningless bullshit, things they thought mattered but didn't. A woman cut across the stairs and then stutter-stepped, trying to figure out which way to get past me. My head raised and it was you. You wearing a bubble winter coat, a few inches shorter, twenty pounds heavier. You with blond hair and deep wrinkles around your mouth. But you, until your face sank below the surface, leaving a stranger's face in its place, scared eyes circling me until she left.

I reached out for the hand railing and caught myself. The walls of my stomach clenched.

After you died I saw you in every woman's face. I mistook them for you if I turned too fast or scanned a room. It wasn't that they resembled you. They *were* you. You in a disguise, in a costume, but acting out some other role. They didn't have to resemble you to trigger this. Elderly women, different nationalities, high school girls, a couple of times women in burkas. I could feel my pupils expand like a drop of blood in water. Your face would fade back into theirs within seconds, and I'd be left immobile and struggling to compose myself.

I got to the landing before the next flight of stairs and stopped. This was where your head hit the ground and the witness described it as hearing "A loud pop, like a bowling pin."

The only thing that came close to capturing what life

felt like with you dead was that a part of my physical body was gone now. Lopped off. There on the landing, I felt the throb of where the missing piece had fallen.

Everyone who had gotten off at this stop had filed past me. I walked up to the platform. From there I could see our building, the rest of 18th lit up. Standing on the platform with me was a lanky, dark-haired man, someone who could have been my uncle Eddie, the one who went to high school with your mom. He was wearing an oversize jacket and dingy black pants covered in dust and paint, his boots the same. Dark skinned, thick coarse hair he had combed lazily. He noticed me staring at him and looked away. He moved farther down the platform.

Something turned in the kiln fire, rustling embers that carried into my chest. I couldn't help but think who he was on his way to kill.

His whole miserable life played out in my head. He worked menial jobs just to get by, but he and his wife still brought kid after kid into this world, because God told them to be fruitful and multiply, but he never said anything about raising them, so the kids floated through the neighborhood, latching on to whatever role models they could find, too weak to forge a way for themselves, and they would grow up to kill us, and leech off our resources until we fell into the pit with them, naked bodies climbing over one another, the dog kennel cries of misery and despair.

These thoughts passed through me like a voice only I could hear.

Push, the voice whispered. Not a man's or woman's voice. Not even speaking in words, so much as an urge, an insistence I was finding harder to deny. *Push him.*

He was looking around the platform. *Looking for victims*, the voice observed. In his hand was a cell phone. I could feel the voice caress my neck. *Who did he steal it from?*

I felt one foot move in front of the other. The tracks were to my left, greased and slick, reflecting the overhead lights.

"Attention," an automated voice announced over the speakers. "An inbound train toward the Loop will be arriving in one minute."

All around me, blackness closed in on this man, and it was like I was watching myself as I stepped closer to him. Not a participant anymore, but an observer.

In this headspace, all around me was shadow, and in the shadow, I could feel something else.

The train's lights were growing in intensity as it approached the station. After cowering away from me, the man checked to see if I was still looking at him, and I was, and the fear in his eyes pulled me back into myself. The headspace and its darkness disappeared, and I was in my body again, behind the controls again.

More people stepped between us. I stopped. I couldn't remember my last thought. Or I did, but I didn't want to admit it to myself then. The insistence that was engorging my muscles with blood seconds ago was suddenly a fading memory, a dream of a time when I had felt powerful and unsparing. Capable of anything. I could hardly look in his direction anymore. The rush of air as the train entered the station caught me off guard. I whipped around and startled the commuters behind me. The train doors opened and a flood of people spilled out. I let the current take me.

Diane texted me, asking if I was heading to the cemetery on Sunday. This was going to be a thing now, either going to the cemetery with your parents or going on my own and confirming with her that I did. At least if I went on my own I could bring a book or listen to music, sit on the grass at least. Better than standing with your mom before the rectangle of grass that's just a shade darker than the other grass around it, staring down at your grave, both of us silent and somber, the whole time I'm waiting for your mom to give the signal that we can leave, we've sufficiently paid our respects and now you can't hate us or God can't hold it against us, at least for one more week.

Your grave turned into a bookmark we couldn't get past. That we kept going back to. You.

Something you would have gotten a kick out of: the debt you were so keen on eliminating from school and credit cards, we don't have to pay it anymore. I mean me. The lawyer at your job clued me in on this. Since you didn't have an estate, and the truck was in my name, debt collectors had nothing to go after. Even the credit cards we both used but that you opened, I could let them default. Like you couldn't die and just let me fend for myself. You had to make sure the slate would be wiped clean for me too, so maybe I could start a new life. It's what we who are bereaved like to call "settling affairs," only you were doing it for me from beyond the grave, like you knew I would be too busy trying to crawl into the casket to sweat the small stuff.

Tacked on the fridge was the postcard with Fidelia Marroquín's new address. I don't know why I saved it. I hardly remembered putting it up there. Every time I went for something to eat, there was her name, her address. Only five blocks away from where we lived.

I only mailed the envelope because you wanted to talk to this woman. Maybe she knew how to get rid of the thing in our home. Maybe she wanted money, or was trying to contact a dead loved one. Maybe if she saw we were the ones suffering, she would take it back. More than anything, you just wanted to know what was happening. So did I.

The stone steps leading down to her garden unit were crumbling at the edges. The curtains were drawn, but a yellow light bled through, the shadows of trinkets and junk on the windowsill.

I exhaled into my palm to see if I could smell the whiskey on my breath and then knocked on the storm door, rattling the whole thing. She didn't answer. I opened the storm door and knocked again. A dark shape shuffled past the windows.

She was almost a foot shorter than my line of sight. Her long gray hair was tied into a neat bun, and she was wearing one of those old-school aprons with ruffles running down the sides. There was something spongy looking about her. Part of me wondered if I poked the flab on her arm would my finger poke through and hit bone. And all of it held together with skin that looked like brown plastic grocery bags.

"Sí?"

"Fidelia Marroquín?" I said. Her name sounded so awkward in my mouth, my tongue tripping over what would have sounded like silk coming from you.

The softness in her face receded and something a little more wary replaced it. Her eyebrows were mostly gone, so when they bunched together the black of her pupils stood out more, overtaking the eyes. A blank, lifeless gaze. "Qué quieres?"

I did my best to tell her I lived in her old building. Whenever I have to talk in Spanish, it always feels like I'm caught in a raging river and the few words I understand

and use are flotsam I can hold on to until it's my turn again to talk and I need the next word. "Sabes . . . si . . . algo . . . pasó . . . en el . . . edificio? Algo mal? Cucuy?"

She nodded through my choppy Spanish. A smile spread under her beady doll eyes.

She said something too fast for me to piece together, but when she stepped aside, I knew she was asking me to come inside.

The wood-paneled walls and dark carpeting made the space feel dreary. She couldn't have been there for more than a year, about as long as we were in the condo, but she had accumulated a good amount of junk already, piles of clothes and old newspapers, the kitchen counter covered with aluminum cans and glass jars. A hoarder.

I stood next to her couch but didn't sit. Her Spanish was a ribbon trailing behind her as she moved into the kitchen, talking and talking and talking, none of it sticking to me even remotely. She sounded comfortable enough with me, though. I learned to pay attention to tone at a young age, so if I couldn't catch up to the words, at least I could tell if I was getting yelled at or not. And Fidelia, she sounded grandmotherly, a singsong rhythm in her voice. She returned with two cups of tea and sat mine on the edge of the coffee table covered with tabloid magazines. Bits of grounds and sticks sat at the bottom of the mug. I didn't drink it.

She sat in her recliner and the momentum rocked her back and forth slightly, but the mug held close to her chest never spilled. I knew I wasn't going to understand everything she said, but I hoped she would speak slowly enough for me to translate in my head as we went. The singsong rhythm in her voice changed to something more accusatory.

"Fijate como [something something something]?" She waved her right arm to draw my eyes to the apartment. She wanted me to see how she was living. "Entonces [something something] el Cucuy?" Which in English was basically the boogeyman.

She smiled. "Pero no es el Cucuy." So it wasn't the boogeyman in our condo. "Los gringos [something something] para saber que pasa cuando [something else]." By gringos, she had to be talking about the real estate agent, and the buyer, Mr. Groff.

I was interpreting the words I could understand the way a fortune-teller would read the sediment in my cup of tea. It seemed like she wanted to get back at Mr. Groff for forcing her into this place, and apparently what was in our home wasn't the boogeyman. If she had told me what it was, then it was lost in the words I didn't understand.

I sat on the edge of the couch. "Mataste el animal?" Did you kill the animal?

She shook her head and started talking like I had misunderstood, but I was absolutely drowning in her words. She seemed to enjoy watching me struggle. When I tried to chime in and say, *Qué?* she wouldn't repeat herself.

She leaned forward in her recliner and pointed at me,

but she didn't look angry. The way her eyes bulged and her over-enunciation of each word reminded me of my father when he was drunk, pointing at me and telling me all the things I was doing wrong in life. It sounded as though she were laying everything she had done at my feet including what to do next, maybe because she knew I wouldn't understand it. A dull sensation rippled over my brain.

"Por qué?" I said, cutting her off. "Los gringos no . . . viven . . . en la casa. Solo yo . . . y mi esposa. Somos Mexicanos. No somos tu . . . tu . . . enemy . . . enemigo."

"Mijo," she said, setting her cup down. And then she dropped the hammer. "Tú no eres Mexicano."

You are not Mexican. It was the same thing I heard all my life. When I was eleven and told my dad the food was too spicy, and he looked at me disgusted and said, "What kind of Mexican are you?" When a kid at school heard me stumble through Spanish: "You ain't Mexican." The thing everyone held over me. I might have a squeaky clean record, I might have gone to college, I might be married and have my own condo, but at least they were Mexicans, real Mexicans. And I was not. And Fidelia, who I'd never met before in my life, was throwing the same bullshit back at me.

She opened her hand and spread her nubby fingers over her face. "Es una máscara." My face, in Fidelia's eyes, was a mask.

I stood up, my hands balled into fists. "What the fuck did you do to my home? What is it?" I still couldn't bring myself to call it out, to put a name on it that would give people the ammo to call me crazy. *Did you hear the things Thiago's been claiming? Poor kid.*

Fidelia kept talking, but my concentration was slipping, and the words and their meaning drifted past me. I caught "Canal" and "Nunca va . . ." before her head bowed to her chest, and she sat looking into her cup.

Canal Street was on the other side of the expressway. "Is there something on Canal?" I said. "Are you telling me to go there?"

Her shoulders slumped and she shook her head. "Aye, niño," she said, the words laced with pity.

Rain pattered against the windows. I turned to leave. I opened the door and smelled the warm scent of drizzle.

"No end," Fidelia said from the apartment.

"Que, no end?" I said. "No end what?"

She looked into her cup and said it again, the words unfamiliar in her mouth. "No end. No end."

The light fixture in the kitchen began to flicker, and I left.

"Are you sleeping?"

I was home, lying in bed but on top of the comforter, and the couple upstairs were fighting again. Which meant the bars were closed, which meant it was late. Diane sounded drunk over the phone. She didn't wait for me to respond.

"No one understands," she said. "They keep talking about time. You need time, it'll take time. Like I'll get over her and everything will go back to normal. I don't want to get over anything, Thiago. I want to sink as far as it'll take me."

A haze of light glowed outside our bedroom door. It was coming from the living room and running down the hall.

My first thought was Itza, but there was a red tint blinking over the white light. Maybe traffic was backed up in front of our place. Maybe it was an ambulance.

"They don't understand and now you're leaving me too," she said.

I had decided to use the insurance money and move as far away as I could without actually becoming a cave dweller. Estes Park was a small town nestled in the Colorado mountains. I found a listing online for a pretty decent cabin and put in an offer. None of your friends knew where I was going. I gave all of your belongings to Diane, with the exception of your beat-up Ugg boots, a pair of earrings I bought you for Christmas, and the official commemorative teacup of Prince Harry and Meghan Markle's wedding.

"Mr. Diaz understands," I said. "Vera was his daughter too."

"Not a biological one. Don't tell him I said that. Anyway, he's just like them. Phase talk. That's all they're good for. They don't know what it's like, not like you." The receiver rubbed against something, maybe falling from her face, and I could hear her heaving a tired cry, a sort of exhausted weep I also knew.

"How can you move so far when you know she's here? She's buried here."

"Some of her is buried here," I said. "The rest I don't know. I have to get out of here or I'll go crazy. People want to use her for their own means, like she's a prop to their story."

Everything was poisoned. People who knew nothing about me needed my comment on an article, wanted me to be interviewed, our Facebook photos popping up on TV next to talking heads. Our honeymoon photo in the newspaper. I needed to go, or the world did.

"You leave me no choice, Thiago. I have to do it."

"Do what?"

"Ask what would Vera think of this."

I smiled, which I think is what she was going for. She must have had the same question lobbed at her enough times for her to know how meaningless it was. It only proved the emptiness of words. How many coworkers had asked Diane the same thing at the bar, after she'd gotten so wasted they had to call your stepdad to pick her up? *What would Vera think?* That's what your memory had become. A way to keep us in line.

"That's easy," I told her. "She'd think I was dumb for picking the mountains over somewhere warm, like a deserted island, nothing but white sand and water as far as you could see. If it was the other way around, that's where she would go."

"I'm gonna miss you, kid."

"You've got the address," I said. "Come visit."

She hung up. I got out of bed, lured to the reddish light.

It was a redder glow farther down the hall, toward the living room. On the edge of the TV stand, Itza was blinking. The white hexagon pattern spun the way it did when she was searching for an answer. The spinning stopped, and the lines between the hexagons pulsed red.

"I'm having trouble locating that for you," she said.

The people upstairs were arguing. I could hear them pacing back and forth, screaming at each other. Maybe that had triggered her.

"Itza, off."

Again the rotation of the soccer ball, but instead of shutting down, the light collapsed into one hexagon, where it located my voice.

"You keep using that word," she said. "I do not think it means what you think it means."

I froze. The adrenaline spike pushed my shoulders back, alert. I had heard that line before, but I couldn't remember where.

"Itza," I said, "where's that line from?"

The orb searched, then: "You can't handle the truth."

I got that one.

The muffled sound of a door slamming upstairs meant the fight was probably over. Itza switched off and left me standing in the dark. After a couple seconds of no sound, I started to walk away and the orb lit up again, somehow brighter.

"You take the blue pill—the story ends, you wake up in your bed and believe whatever you want to believe. You take the red pill—you stay in Wonderland and I show you how deep the rabbit hole goes."

Before I could say anything the hexagons were spinning again, a single one stopping in the direction of where I stood, even though I hadn't said anything.

"How I wonder what you are," she sang in a singsong voice.

"Itza," I said, "mute."

"I'm sorry, Dave. I'm afraid I can't do that."

It was a malfunction, a stuck trigger. I knew she was programmed for pop culture quotes. That mechanism was obviously going haywire. I went toward Itza and her blinding light as she spun again, solid beams of ultra-white blooming in all directions. I was going to reach behind the TV stand and pull the cord from the outlet.

The spinning stopped and collapsed again into a single hexagon, but it wasn't pointed at me. It was pointing to the left of me, the other end of the living room.

There was something there, in the shadows beyond Itza's glow. Not a person. It didn't have the shape of anything I recognized. The only certainty was that whatever it was, it made that corner darker than anywhere else in the room.

"May you ride eternal," Itza said. "Shiny and chrome."

The final hexagon died out, turning the whole room dark. The floorboards in that far corner squeaked under the weight of something.

I listened to myself say, "Hello?"

I took a step back and waited to hear the floorboards creak again. The sound of blood sloshed in my ears. Oceans of blood.

Whoever had slammed the door upstairs, they had just swung it open.

"AND ANOTHER THING—"

I heard the heavy thud of feet charging toward me. I screamed, backpedaling until I tripped over myself and fell. My back hit the wall, knocking a picture frame off its nail. The glass shattered on the floor.

As quick as they'd rushed forward, the footsteps were gone. I got up and grabbed a knife from the block on the counter. I turned on all the lights in the rooms, opening the closets, checking under the bed, the bathroom, pulling back the curtain. But there was nothing, no one.

The white orb was off when I went back into the living room, but it still felt like she—it—was looking at me.

I was so done with this thing. I pushed the stand away from the wall and pulled the plug. If this thing could only fucking work right. A stupid fucking alarm that somehow reached across time and space to switch the tracks to our lives. This thing didn't deserve a second life on eBay or Craigslist.

The next morning I wedged it against the front tire of our truck and reversed over it, slowly, with the windows down, so I could listen to its shell fracture.

II.

The drive through Iowa and Nebraska was the same as the drive through western Illinois. Pretty much as soon as I left the city limits everything on either side of the highway embankments looked the same: cornfields that gave way to rolling, bare plains.

The sky somehow doubled itself, able to stretch out once the buildings and skyscrapers fell back. The whole sky was that floor-model TV with top-of-the-line clarity, so sharp and vibrant that it felt like I could reach up and switch the equilibrium of the earth, fall into the sky and swim in that ocean of Downy. Big Lovecraftian clouds moved below the blue expanse, bigger than I could comprehend. My eyes immediately trying to categorize their shape into a recognizable form. They made me feel small and alone, but those feelings didn't come with sadness. The herd of clouds moving over the road took the spotlight off me. In the city, around humans, I was someone. But out here, I was an ant.

At night there was only the road, the few feet of it shown in the headlights. The road split into single lanes of traffic with a median strip of dead grass in the middle, not that it mattered. I hadn't seen a single car or truck since time crossed over to the other side of midnight.

Both cup holders in the center console had empty paper cups stained with coffee, and I was hungry and driving with a full bladder. The last oasis was at least two podcasts ago. A Google search for anything nearby buffered for a long time before it read the page could not open. After a while there weren't even the marble eyes of deer along the road. It felt as though I'd passed over into somewhere not meant for me. A back lot to nature. The stripped farm plains in the night, the wide expanse, took on a lunar surface.

The signal bars on my phone counted down—three, two, one. The Maps app disabled. It had happened before and most of the time it would refresh a few miles up the road. I closed and opened the app, restarted my phone, but the GPS kept searching for my location. Signs for an interstate I maybe needed to take were posted along the shoulder. Two miles. One mile. Exit-only lane.

"Fuck!"

Once the overpass was in my rearview mirror, the road felt different. I stopped getting passed by the running lights along semitrucks. No headlights in my rearview mirror. I obviously needed to make that turn, which was what my gut told me. Except my gut had never been to Colorado so what the fuck did it know.

Another exit finally appeared along the road. A dented white sign, different from the green highway ones, that read, OASIS. I pulled off at the exit.

Along the road was a gravel shoulder, so I stopped, opened the driver's-side door and pissed my brains out. After that I sort of just drove, checking the mileage to see how far I had gone without seeing anything that remotely looked like an oasis, telling myself I'd drive six miles before turning back around. It wasn't until the shadows broke that I noticed I'd driven past a mass of something, trees maybe. The shadows sort of peeled back the way a movie screen will extend wider after the trailers finish. A parking lot appeared next to the road. Beyond the empty parking spots, a diner.

This place was five miles from the exit, and even though I'd made up my mind on six miles being the limit, this still felt too far to be the kind of place that welcomed travelers. It could turn out to be a local hole in the wall hostile to new people. Read: minorities.

I pulled into a spot in front if only to turn back around if I needed to bolt. The diner's facade was all glass and the interior was lit up. Empty. It was so bright I could hardly see the white brick of the building. Inside, there were red leather booths, a long white counter across from where customers first entered, all the stools empty. Past the counter was a pop machine, one of those metal churners where they blend ice cream. There were stacks of glasses and dishes and a view to the kitchen, where everything was stainless steel. But no sign outside the place.

A man in a white paper hat and white cook's apron pushed through a set of double doors. I watched him hit a few keys on the cash register and the drawer opened.

It was either this to try and get directions, or test my luck farther down the road. I shifted into park and headed for the door.

The sudden movement outside must have spooked him. His head shot up and we locked eyes for a brief second, enough time for me to run a simulation in my head. One where I just turned back around and left. His bulbous eyes and gaunt face weirded me out, but if I just left, then maybe he would think I was trying to rob him and had chickened out. Maybe this was the only time he had ever seen a Mexican before, and here was my chance to sway his views with a positive experience.

The door dinged and I stepped inside, my shoes squeaking against the red-and-white-checkered floor.

"Howdy," I said. Fucking *howdy*. Out of these lips.

"What's up?" he said, moving a rack of clean dishes. Under the apron he wore a white T-shirt. He looked old, but with a boyish pop to his expressions and gestures—the way guys look when they don't have any kids. He was less skinny than he was ropy, huge hands to match his Frankenstein head.

I asked if he was open. It took him a second to answer. He pulled the key out of the register and flipped off the light switch that displayed the pies.

"That's a very loaded question," he said. He looked pre-occupied, and I was more than happy to leave him with his thoughts. "I'm sorry," he said. "I'm open but I was just about to close. I'm open but I'm trying to sell this place too, you get what I mean?"

"Random question, but you wouldn't happen to know how to get to Colorado, would you? My phone can't get a signal out here."

It didn't surprise him. The cell phone companies for-got about this place the same way everyone else did. "I'm guessing you got off at I-80 a few miles back. Take it going west and it should get you to I-76. That'll get you into Col-orado. Hopefully by then your phone works. Otherwise vaya con Dios."

I thanked him.

"My grill's off," he said when I went to leave. "But I can make you a milkshake. On the house."

He pulled the rag off the counter but I didn't sit. He bent and pulled out a gallon of milk, a can of whipped cream, a brown bottle of extract. "You like chocolate?"

"Sure."

He walked to the far end of the counter and grabbed some more ingredients. "The state released their plans for a highway," he said, "and my dad bought this place according to the prospective blueprints. It wasn't until construction started that some farmer refused to sell his land and they had to move the highway five miles out. My dad did all right, but I can't compete with the big chains damn near built over the highways."

"That's rough," I told him.

He scooped out the chocolate ice cream and squeezed off the scoops into a steel mixer. He poured out the milk without measuring, adding chocolate chips and crushed cookies. "Figures that as soon as he set down money, the interstate would shift away. Sometimes it seems like the whole world is against you." He kicked on the mixer and the metal wand churned in slow, even circles. "What's that saying about God and making plans and him laughing at you?"

I couldn't remember how it went, but I told him I knew what he was talking about.

"It's enough to make a man think he's Job," he said. The way he looked at me, eyes burning, it was like he was giving me all the attention in the world.

"Yeah," I said, not sure what else to say.

For being in the family two generations, the place looked immaculate. There had to be a renovation somewhere in those years, except according to him, it was a money pit. The stool cushions looked untouched, not a butt groove or crease in the row. For a split second I thought I saw blue sky in my peripheral, coming from the left of the diner. I turned but the windows only reflected the interior lights, darkness beyond the glass, like God had flicked the sun on and off thinking none of us would notice. That blueness didn't feel like an illusion though. It had the feel of a memory, as fast as it came and went. The more I turned it over in my head, the more I thought I had seen a blue horizon, the sky touching the ocean. There was moss outside the window. I thought I heard waves crashing against rocks.

Lack of sleep. That's what I chalked it up to. I was trying to fit over 1,100 miles into one straight shot, no motel rooms, no breaks except for gas and restrooms. After the first ten hours I kept catching myself zoning out on the straight road, hypnotized, and I wouldn't snap out of it until half an album was over or the Maps app announced an upcoming merge. My mind was just loopy.

"You start to question what it was you did to bring all this on," the cook said, "like maybe it's all your fault."

He grabbed a plastic to-go cup and set it on the counter. He bent down and his eyes hovered above the rim as he swirled the chocolate syrup around the inside. "You ever see that movie where the people can run on walls and dodge bullets? And they live in that video game?" His eyes closed briefly as he shivered. "Freaked me the hell out. Because how would you ever know you're in it? How would you even know to fight it? So you didn't pour all your savings into a place just for the damn programmer to put the highway five miles from where it's supposed to be . . ."

If I knew he was going to get into his life troubles, I would have skipped on the free shake. My appetite was

gone and all I wanted to do was leave before he started crying and showing me pictures of his kids or some shit.

"Or what if it's not the world, but some other *thing* doing all this to you?" He unlatched the steel mixing cup,
poured it into the syrup-swirled to-go cup. "Some kinda
force, or entity. Evil, all-powerful. Controls everything. Got
you in a spell-like. Can alter math and change logic so that
the sky, the air, the earth, colors, shapes, and sounds, all
external things are merely the delusions of dreams devised
to ensnare your judgment."

"Uh, and why would it want to do that?"

He pushed the shake across the counter and shrugged.
"Maybe this thing hates it where it is. Where it's been for
millennia. Not dead but sure as shit not alive either, and it
can't get out. Maybe he's desperate. Maybe you got something he wants, and the only way to get it is if you willingly
give it up. So maybe he's gonna have to trick you."

I reached for the milkshake, just trying to get out of
there.

"Wait a sec." He grabbed my wrist, moving so fast I
could barely process it, his hand ice cold against my skin,
so intense that it burned. The fear rose up in me so fast I
thought I would scream, but he let go just as fast, making
the whole thing feel imagined. He popped a lid on the cup
before reaching out with the shake and a straw. "All yours,
boss."

I made like I was adjusting my jacket sleeve and rubbed
the skin where he touched me. My wrist felt fine, more

proof that my brain was running on fumes. Maybe I really was hungry. Maybe the cook's strange vibe was all in my head.

I asked him, if something could do all that, why couldn't it just take a person whenever it wanted?

"Shit, I don't know. You ever seen them scary movies? Possession makes a mess of everything. The person gets all fucking torn to shreds. But a body freely given?"

"I'm pretty sure this is Descartes's whole shtick," I said.

"What is?"

"Some kind of evil genius or spirit that's tricking you. That's how he got to the 'I think therefore I am' line. Maybe he was being tricked, but at least he knew he had to *exist* to be tricked."

His bottom lip swallowed the top one as he nodded with his head cocked. "News to me. 'Genius' is your word by the way, but I like it."

I tried to pay him but he wouldn't take it. I thanked him and he just looked at me with his arms at his sides.

The door dinged on my way out. I unlocked my car doors, and when I looked back, the cook was still wiping down the counter, which had looked clean to me when I was standing there. I took two or three quick pulls to get the shake down to a level so it wouldn't spill over in the cup holder. It was good, thick and chocolaty, but balanced with the milk. The best milkshake I maybe ever had.

I pulled out of the lot and got back on the road. I headed toward the highway, sipping on the shake, already feeling rejuvenated. The plan was still to drive to Estes Park without stopping to sleep and it felt like that was going to happen.

A shape, something small and low to the ground, crept out of the dark of the shoulder and into my headlights. I slammed on the brakes for what turned out to be a torn garbage bag, its frayed end whipping in the air when my eyes caught it.

Call it muscle memory. A lifetime of city traffic, watching the brake lights of the car ahead suddenly grow bigger in the windshield. It's not enough to brake. Everyone knows the second part is immediately looking into the rearview mirror, to see the car behind barreling forward, hoping they saw in time and have enough space to brake, or the wherewithal to swerve into the shoulder or the next lane.

I braked, the whole car frame lurched forward, jerked back, and my eyes veered to the rearview mirror, looking for the oncoming car I knew wasn't there but I couldn't stop myself.

I saw it. I know I saw it. But as quick as my eyes darted to the mirror, it was gone.

I'll freely admit the cook scared me, with his bruised eyes and knobby hands. For the rest of the drive, I kept telling myself it was one of those things the brain does. When it sees something it can't compute, it stretches an old reference over the thing like a costume, something you can recognize.

It wasn't even a full look. All of it was semiautomatic fast.

In the rearview mirror I saw the red glow of the brake lights on the blacktop, and out of the dead night something scrambled, like an animal, into the red. It was crawling on all fours, except its legs were spread out on either side of its body like a spider. A spider the size of a person. Its hind legs were covered in denim, something white flapping under its belly, what could have been the cook's apron. His eyes had completely fallen into his head, leaving two yawning gapes.

I glanced at the rearview mirror again and then really looked into it to make sure I saw what I saw, but it was gone.

My foot hit the gas anyway. I was getting used to parts of me operating on their own. The back end of the truck fishtailed. Exhaust smoke filled the space where the cook-thing had been. The truck jerked forward and then punched it, speeding toward the highway.

By the time daylight returned, I'd forgotten all about it.

But it was him. I know that now.

It wasn't until I hit Boulder that the snow-covered plains with jutting rocks fell away, and for-real mountains burst from the ground and climbed into the sky. The forests drew in on the road. The sky narrowed between the treetops to leave a crisp stripe of blue. The road cut through a national park and opened again into a valley of mountain ranges—a landscape God kept in the back. The scenery like a sloppily frosted cake. Colorado was already beyond what I could have hoped.

Black trees bunched up the slopes except for the bald summits that pushed higher into the clouds.

I told myself this was where I lived now.

It was the opposite of what everyone wanted for me. They said I needed to throw myself into work, keep myself busy, not be a stranger. Friends we hung out with for years asked for my number. They just assumed I would fill the role you had inhabited for them so naturally. I'd be that person for them in their lives now. That easy.

To them, for me to move to a cabin in the mountains, where I didn't know a single person, had no job, it was like I was giving up. They were goddamn right.

The pageantry was over. Not just for the cameras. For all of it. I tried dropping the charges against Esteban, to make the case go away, but that only happens in the movies; prosecutors file charges, not victims. Diane wanted Esteban *under* the prison, but she at least got why I wanted it done and over with, more than I could say for your friends and cousins, but they didn't matter anymore. You enjoyed people, and I knew spending my life with you would mean parties, get-togethers, couples dates, but that was all gone now. When you died I mourned you, but also the version of myself I was with you. So there were two deaths.

I saw the house just off the road, in a basin surrounded by landscape: trees and rocks and steep slopes. I turned onto a small gravel road that also acted as my driveway, the one-way path splitting a curtain of trees preceding the property. At the far end of the path was the cabin. Behind it was a clearing, a few hundred yards of bare land covered in snow before another wall of pines took over, what led to the Rocky Mountain National Park.

I knew this all from the real estate agent. In an email he said I should get ready for hunters knocking down my door, asking for permission to retrieve their kill off my land if in its last efforts it collapsed on my property. Legally, the kill would belong to me, he said. If the hunter was an asshole, I should by all means refuse his entering. Most people wanted to keep on good terms with landowners, so oftentimes hunters would give me free meat if I wanted. He also said on clear days I could see Grays Peak, the highest point on the Continental Divide.

The cabin was this reddish-amber wood and had a brick chimney and a gray pitched roof, the kind of place every four-year-old can draw as a stand-in for their home.

The agent was sitting in his truck, and when he saw me turn onto the path, he got out and waved.

I grabbed my suitcase. The agent walked to the door, waiting for me under the porch light, holding out the keys and jingling them. But the cabin had a big front window, and I could see the whole place was lit up from the inside, meaning he had gone in and turned on the lights and then locked the door again, like it was really important for me to believe I was the first to open the door.

"Congratulations on your new home," he said. "Ready to step into it for the first time?"

He was in a better mood than the first time we talked.

His office was highly rated in online reviews. I'd told him I wanted to buy a place and gave him one specification: it had to be away from people.

I think he figured this was some kind of gag some of his real estate buddies were pulling, a buyer who wanted a fully furnished cabin with utilities ready to go, who didn't want to fly in to see what else was available, who was willing to waive an inspection, and wanted to pay in cash. When he found this place and sent me the link, an asking price at the high end of my budget, he was happier than I was when I said I'd take it, no mortgage to worry about.

The condo sold at a gain too. Think of all the frozen pizzas that could buy.

The whole cabin was fitted with oversize windows, taking full advantage of the blue mountains, the pattern of snow sitting in tree branches, mountains in every room we looked out of, like we were sitting in the bald spot of a king's crown. In the living room was a huge fireplace, on either side was a pair of shelves with books on them, spy novels and classics. The ceiling was vaulted, a network of wooden beams that looked sturdy enough for someone to hang themselves.

"Real books?" I said, and took one off and flipped through the pages, words and everything, not hollowed out with a flask in it. Across from the living room was the kitchen with a woodburning stove, a breakfast bar separating the rooms. To the left were French doors that opened onto a small wooden patio where the agent said I could watch the deer while sipping my coffee. Upstairs were the two bedrooms, a full bath, closet, blah blah blah. Four walls and a roof. And very, very far from home.

"You got a moving company meeting you here?" the agent said, as I pulled the cork out of the wine bottle he left in the gift basket for me.

"It's on the way," I lied, offering him the first swig of the red wine. He shook his head.

He left and I stood with the bottle in front of the French doors and looked out at the expanse of nature, the deep forest staring back at me. The pine needles were such a dark green that on the branch they looked black. The trees so packed together they looked like one big organism.

The wine warmed my stomach. Outside the sky blazed orange as the sun set and the trees faded from a heavy green into a charred black. The plateglass in the doors shook from the wind. From what the agent said, Colorado weather didn't seem all that different from Chicago weather. The cold hit hard and there would be no mercy, because it was incapable of mercy. There was no working part of it to be appeased. And no amount of gear could keep the chill from piercing the skin, setting into the bones. Stay out long enough and no down jacket or thermal socks could save a person from what was coming for them. The weather was to be endured, not conquered.

An owl flew over the cabin and swept into the tree line. I stepped aside for you to see and then remembered you were dead.

At the wake, the funeral, everyone paid their respects to your parents sitting in the front pew and then walked to the back of the church and collapsed into my arms. They told me you appeared in their dreams. These were friends and extended family, but also coworkers you always bitched about at home. People you barely hung out with, who you barely liked, yet suddenly you were in their dreams, standing in a meadow and smiling, telling them you were okay now.

Tía Cheeky pulled me into her chest and said she heard you in her house, walking from room to room. "I lit a candle and helped her cross to the other side."

If she only knew how we felt about her plastic-covered furniture, the Precious Moments figurines in the bathroom, the way she cut your uncle down in front of company.

The first couple times people told me you had visited them and told them you found peace, I smiled and said something about how reassuring that was, but inside I was ripping the wallpaper off my skull.

As a kid I spent most of my summers on the basketball court, so many two-on-twos and full-courts and twenty-ones that at night I would dream about dribbling and passing the ball and would smash my knuckles against the bedroom wall. It was obvious what these dreams were. A digestion of the waking day. Twelve hours of dribbling a ball, what else would I dream about? Stunned by your death, unable to believe it, of course they'd construct some fantasy where you were alive and reassuring *them*, because even in death your obligation to other people wasn't finished.

At the same time, I waited for my own dreams. By all means, brain, delude me.

But you never showed. No assurance that you were okay, no floating away in a ball of light, no guarantee that we would see each other again.

Seeing everyone else scramble for meaning left me cold. I didn't allow anything in me that would make me look foolish or desperate, and I closed the door on my brain's ability to craft a dream meant to comfort me and provide me with the only thing I truly wanted: to see you again.

Under the deck was a bundle of firewood covered with a tarp. I took a couple pieces and threw them in the fireplace, doused them with lighter fluid because what the fuck did I know. I burned my hand opening the vent after smoke filled the living room and the flames licked the edges of the brick.

I had the intention of listening to some music, but the snap and crack of the fire suited me better, sitting on the floor and leaning on my suitcase, feet toward the fire. The world outside grew darker and darker until the windows revealed nothing but blackness, nothing to see but my own reflection.

I don't even like wine.

As the flames shrank, that moonless dark made its way inside the cabin. I figured Colorado nights would gleam like gems on a jeweler's velvet display, but the need to go outside and look couldn't override how comfortable I felt curled on my side, the empty bottle clutched to my chest. The last few licks of fire retreated into the used-up wood. I opened my eyes and only the embers were left, holding on, glowing with all that dark around us.

The dry heaving woke me up. I opened my eyes to the feel of puke rushing up my throat. I scrambled to my feet, tripped over my suitcase, felt around the breakfast bar and projectiled into the sink. Between the heaves was a desperate, all-consuming need for water. Water.

Chalk it up to forgetting my new home was over seven thousand feet above sea level. The oxygen had been squeezing out of my blood, and what did I do but attach a NOS tank to the whole process by downing a bottle of wine.

Once my throat and nostrils cleared I turned on the faucet, lapping at the cold water, not totally sure if tap water here was safe but not caring either. With my head cocked sideways to get under the tap, I could see the front door facing me at the far end of the hall. Its frame was completely illuminated in light, like the window in our bedroom when the upstairs guy would start his car.

So this was a dream, because only in my dreams did this happen. But once I figured it out, the dream didn't pull apart like cotton candy. The doorway of light stayed, but I knew I was dreaming, I knew, and I walked toward the door knowing that I could make whatever I wanted happen. There could be a beach outside the door if I wanted. I could fly. I could see you.

In our condo, I would wake up when I tried to turn the knob and felt the curtain. Here, I turned the knob and felt the bolt turn in the latch.

The door opened to a dense forest. Trees literally a foot away, like the state park organism had grown up to the door in the few hours I was here.

It was day. A gray light pushed through the branches, enough for me to see my feet step onto the snow and not feel anything. Scarves of fog ebbed a few feet off the ground.

I somehow knew that if I kept moving farther into the woods I would find you. Something was transmitting, and I was the antenna picking up the signal. As soon as my hand touched the bark of a tree I passed, your location was relayed to me, like the trees were communicating to each other, watchers taking an interest in helping me. I called out your name and expected you to appear from behind a tree. I kept expecting you to step out of thin air, like the world was a green screen you'd figured out how to manipulate.

I ran through the snow, zigzagging toward the edge of the forest but never reaching it. I kept trying to will you into existence. Squeeze my eyes shut and there you would be. Swing myself around and you would run into my arms.

I stopped running and screamed your name but nothing came out. My voice was muted, and what followed it wasn't a sound exactly, but a pressure, the way the last few seconds of holding your breath underwater has a ring to it.

The sound shuddered through the forest, shaking the snow off branches. The ground trembled beneath my feet. It echoed to the edge of the forest where it faded and died. A silence followed, and then the sound reverberated back. More powerful, with more force than I could ever muster.

It was the sound of something coming. And whatever it was, I knew it had come from the edge of the forest. It heard me call your name, and now it knew where I was.

The memory of the dream was buried beneath my hangover. It was lost on me when I got up in the morning and rinsed out the wine bottle to fill it with water.

One thing I did pack was our French press. Because weekend mornings, remember? There was a coffee mug in the gift basket, and I poured a cup and looked out the doors, at the clearing that led into the woods. I watched and sipped. The coffee pooled in my mouth because I thought I saw something. There was movement between the trees. I wasn't sure what I expected, but when the doe appeared and scanned the clearing before walking out, the dream returned in an explosion. The details bloomed all at once, not the way a story usually unfolded, but beginning, middle, and end all at the same time, the way stories happened to God.

The closest hardware store Google Maps could find was literally called Hardware Store.

I bought an ax to chop down the bigger blocks of firewood next to the patio. My first chore in this new life: chop the wood. So pure in action and intent. Chop the wood, make heat. There was just the thing and that was it. I reached behind my neck and pulled out a long strand of your hair from my collar.

Standing outside the hardware store was a Saint Bernard. As soon as we locked eyes his gait picked up, tail swinging so hard that his hips fishtailed. He had the typical white-and-reddish-brown coat, one thick white line running down his head to the snout, dividing the two sides of reddish brown that covered his eyes and ears. I looked around for an owner. No one in the hardware store claimed him. A woman sat in her parked car in front of us. She saw the dog and the look on my face and just shrugged.

"Anyone missing a dog?" I called out, and people around us looked but just shook their heads or kept on moving. The sound of my voice made his bushy tail whip faster. He sniffed my crotch and I scooted back. His wet nose stamped the back of my free hand first, then he ducked his head under it, pushing himself into my palm, like I was going to pet him or he was going to get this show started himself. He had that puppy energy buzzing around him, even for being as big as he was. I liked him immediately.

I scratched his neck in the hopes of feeling a collar, but nothing. I dropped my bags off in the trunk and walked with him through the parking lot, asking again if anyone was missing a dog. Maybe there would be a car with an open window he could have crawled out of, maybe a kid darting through the aisles too, looking for his dog, but the cars were sealed up against the cold and no one on the streets looked too concerned, and the whole time this big lug stayed at my side, panting, his jowls staining my pants with drool.

We waited on the sidewalk for anyone to claim him. He took every little movement I made as play, to where I couldn't check my pockets without him trying to sniff inside them. If I shifted my weight he slipped between my legs, arching his head up for affection. His wide orca tongue lapped at the air, trying to lick me.

I went back into the hardware store and bought a canvas drape to keep his fur off the back seat. He waited for me outside.

We drove through town in a big circle, cruising the residential blocks. I'd pull up to a stop sign and the dog would stick his fire hydrant head out of the back window and pedestrians would wave, and I'd ask if they knew anyone missing a Saint Bernard, but they only looked at each other and shrugged, shaking their heads.

In the waiting room to the vet clinic—the only one I could find on my phone—he bobbed his head at the other dogs to get them to play, rolling on his back and whining. The dogs and the owners just looked at him.

"Well, I've never seen him before," Dr. Jacobson said. He scanned him for a chip but didn't find anything. "Doesn't necessarily mean he doesn't belong to anyone. A lot of people don't bring their pets to the vet around here. Usually they're outside dogs that live in a barn or shed."

I asked if there was a shelter around. Maybe his owners would look there first.

"Not in town. Any strays, we're supposed to call the sheriff's office. They transport the dog to the next county. They have a shelter there."

"Could he have wandered from there?"

"Doubt it. He'd have had to follow I-20 through the mountains."

We both stared at the big mop of fur licking my fingers, rolling over for belly rubs. He had no idea how big he was. He probably would try to sleep in my lap if I let him.

"Sweet pup," he said.

"I just don't understand how he popped out of nowhere."

"I'll call the sheriff's and they'll maybe hold him a day or so in case someone comes looking for him."

"The shelter a county over," I said. "Is it a kill shelter?"

Dr. Jacobson touched his finger to the tip of his nose.

"I'll take him, then." It was my voice, but I couldn't believe what I was saying. "If someone comes around, you give me a call. That way he's not a county away."

Dr. Jacobson was nice enough to give me some metal bowls, an extra leash and collar he had in back, a couple cans of wet food until I could transition him to kibble, if it even took that long to find his owners. I left my name and number with the tech up front and came back out, held the door open for the brute, and he lumbered into the truck again, his excited breath sounding deeper in the truck and fogging the windows.

"Well," I said to him, buckling my seat belt, "looks like we're roommates for a while." It felt good to say.

The receptionist had me fill out a form before I could see the doctor. Under *Dog's name*, because of his droopy eyes, hangdog cheeks, and the standing downcast expression on his face, I wrote "Wilford Brimley." And watching him sitting upright in the back seat, his massive head looking out at the world and hearing his tail thump against the cushions, it felt like the name was going to stick.

We hit a few more stores and I drove us home. As soon as I opened the door he walked inside, making for the carpet in the living room. He sniffed it, rolled over, and started rubbing his back, tongue sticking out of his mouth.

I could become the crazy dog man of these parts. Have eight, maybe twelve dogs that crowded around me wherever I went, a parade of tails and floppy ears whenever I opened the back door. Then maybe I'd take up writing. Out in the middle of nowhere, grizzled, I could be one of those serious writers who used ten different words for grass. I would let my hair grow, write, chop the wood, feed the dogs. The days would fill themselves, really.

A part of me always dreamed of this, never having to work again, moving far away from everyone I knew. In the mountains no one was trying to gauge themselves against me. It was just snow, trees, the mountain sky, and the whipped disks of clouds above the peaks. The town below me, well within view. And full of strangers, which was what I wanted. If I was left alone then there was no one for me to hate.

———

Brimley lay on the carpet, gnawing on a Gatorade bottle I stuffed into a sock. Sometimes he stopped to watch me sweat over the plastic inflator that was supposed to pump up this queen-size air mattress. He already set me back a couple dozen pumps after the mattress was starting to take shape and he climbed on top, circling a second before lying down. His weight shot the inflator out of my hands and across the room.

"Goddamn it, Wilford Brimley."

Of course it would make sense to blow up the air mattress in the upstairs bedroom, but I couldn't conceptualize living beyond the living room. This was the cabin with the least square footage of all the ones I saw, and it still felt like the Taj Mahal. The rooms were cavernous. Maybe there had been life here once, but it was hollowed out now. Excavated. What remained was a shell.

Our presence in the living room, though, made the first floor feel soft, the corners of the rooms rounded off. Upstairs, the shadows still clung to the corners like cobwebs, like the dark was the same as heat, rising to the top. At night the rooms felt sharp, lifeless, and if they were filled with anything it was that invisible hostility a person felt in their room after waking up from a bad dream.

The shower was on the second floor, so there was no avoiding that, but now I had backup muscle to follow me up the stairs. He lay on the bathroom tile and kept watch while I showered. Not that I needed it. Not that there was actually something worth guarding against. But if I was grabbing for the shampoo or soap bar or razor I sometimes peeked behind the curtain, and Brimley would be lying down but with his head raised, not growling or barking, but staring intensely at the empty doorway like he heard something.

What Brimley heard was my cell phone, plugged into an outlet downstairs and vibrating on top of the microwave.

After I was dried and dressed, he stood next to the patio doors, lifting his front paws like a soldier marching in place. I took this to mean he was housebroken, so for sure he belonged to someone, which bummed me out a little. Sooner or later his owner would want him back. It took less than a day to get used to having a buddy around. I was pushing on my boots when the phone rang again. I let it go and opened the back door.

Brimley scooted past, running off the patio and bunny-hopping through the snow, dive-bombing into the drifts. He popped back up and his snout was powdered with snow. Half of him was buried when he stopped prancing and hunched over to pop a squat. See you in the spring, poop.

I called him back in and immediately sensed my mistake. What was the word, this sound "Brimley," to a dog I found barely twelve hours ago? He was only with me because he ran from somewhere else. And I could see it in his eyes, the way he looked at me over his shoulder, waiting for the chase, before he turned and bolted for the woods.

Fuck.

I struggled with my coat as I ran after him and the snow

spilled into my boots with each moon step. Any attempt to stay calm fled with Brimley.

"Stop!" I said. "Stay!"

This only made him think we were playing. He paused for a second to make sure I was behind him and then breached the first line of trees.

I followed his snow tracks into the forest, but once he hit dirt the trail faded away. Not that it mattered, because by then I was frantic, running as fast as I could, my untied laces slapping against the trees and my legs, the spearmint air numbing my throat.

The snowfall and tree bark of the whole forest resembled his coat, and the possibility of losing him out there looped in my head. I was supposed to look after him and now he was going to die out here, either from the cold or from some predator. The vet thought I would take care of him like your parents thought I would take care of you. "I've only got the one," your mom said at our wedding. "Treat her good."

Up ahead the ground rose to a steep embankment that blocked Brimley from getting farther away. I caught sight of his floppy ears. To get around it Brimley had to double back and run around the less steep part of the slope. It gave me enough time to catch up, and I was coming in so hot that Brimley cowered at the pounding of my snow-packed boots against the ground. I grabbed his collar, then grabbed the scruff of extra skin on his neck and pulled, twisted.

"Bad dog!"

The yowl he made caused me to let go and spring back. He dropped to the ground and rolled over, tail sweeping the forest floor like a night janitor trying to look busy. One cautious step toward him and he pissed himself, and I wanted to charge face-first into the nearest tree.

Instead of getting closer I just crouched where I was. He stayed in that Spider-Man angle for a beat and then rolled onto his belly, soldier-crawled to me. He dipped his head under my outstretched hand, bobbing against the fingers to get my hand to work, to pet him.

"I'm so sorry, big guy," I said. "That was not cool."

He was too busy licking the air in front of my face to care about the noises accompanying the mouth clouds I was making. I was back in his good graces before I could apologize. Maybe he never put me out. That hurt worst. Even *you* would give me the silent treatment for a day or two. The times we argued because you felt you couldn't invite people to the condo on account of me hating to be "on" all the time, or me wishing you put half as much effort into taking care of yourself as you put into your job. "To do what?" you said, "sit on the couch and watch movies all day with you?" Or the time I wondered out loud if it wasn't our duty as smart people to have children to offset the mouth breathers churning out kids every year, and you floated the idea of getting divorced so I could take on this noble cause unimpeded, because you didn't feel like lugging a living thing in your womb just to have to care for it once it was out. We did our own door-slamming and storming off, talkless nights and quiet mornings because we both had our pride. But there was no putting on airs with Brimley, and it was a brutal way to learn how deep affection tunneled into an animal. To hurt him and see him come back without an ounce of scheming in his eyes.

I'd left the leash back on the kitchen counter, so I unlaced my boots and tied the strings together, tied one end to Brimley's collar. I had a general sense of where we'd entered the forest, except I didn't remember the exposed root coiling out of the ground, the fallen tree beyond that, the glossy stones I could have slipped on, obstacles I must have hurdled to get to the embankment.

Brimley took the lead, sniffing the ground as he headed toward home. The other end of the shoelace was tied around my index finger and already cutting off my circulation.

Maybe because I was too busy minding my footing, trying to keep up with Brimley so the shoelace didn't cut a quarter of my finger off, I didn't see it. Maybe I would have noticed it sooner and steered him in the opposite direction.

Instead, both of our eyes locked on the ground, Brimley's nose practically in the dirt, blowing debris with his nostrils as he followed a mysterious scent, could not stop following it even if he tried.

I was gritting my teeth. "Slow down, buddy." My arm was stretched as far as I could get it.

The scent led him around a tree and the lace bent around its trunk, scraping the bark, shaking the line until it loosened from around my finger and fell.

THIS THING BETWEEN US ❈ 117

But Brimley wasn't running. I hopped around the tree expecting to see his floppy ears getting smaller and smaller ahead of me, but he was right there, his head turned slightly upward at the massive piece of stone standing in front of us, a single slab with perfect ninety-degree corners at the top. The rest of it was webbed with veins of mud, moss, so it was hard to tell if it was all one piece or if the mud was its mortar.

My head went on a swivel and I scanned the woods for the people who had to be watching us, waiting for us to stumble upon this, whatever this was. Either natural instincts or movie instincts told me that this was not a good thing to find.

But there were no faces peeking from behind trees, no cloaked figures, no footprints around the wall from whoever set it there. The base looked so set into the ground that it could have driven into the earth forever. Like on the other side of the world, where its other end erupted from the earth, they built a museum around it and curators detailed its mysterious origins to tourists.

I yelled, "Hello?" Nothing.

Brimley circled the base with his nose to the stone. I followed him around for clues that would explain it. I kept looking off in the direction we came from and then at where we ended up, and there was no way I could have missed this thing as we passed.

It was made of the forest but obviously wasn't of it. I patted my jacket for my phone and remembered it was sitting on the microwave. I stopped circling and just stepped back to take it all in. This wasn't possible. Maybe it was a local thing, an ancient monument they all visited when they were teens, drinking beers in the forest and kicking a ball against the wall.

The wall? Where had I gotten that? It looked more like a giant door, a monolith on the moon. A wall suggested a person couldn't get around it, except Brimley was still circling the base. It must have given off an odd scent for him to be so interested in it. My nose a few inches from the stone, all I could smell was fresh soil.

I grabbed the loose shoestring hanging from Brimley's collar and led him away. It surprised me how much he didn't fight me, like he was done with it too. Every couple of feet I'd turn back to make sure it was still there, to make sure it wasn't any closer. The wall got smaller and smaller behind us until I lost it in the cluster of trees and branches and raised ground.

I told myself I was going to google this when I got home. Or I'd lock Brimley inside and take my phone back out there and snap a photo.

We got back and I had to sit down to pull my shoes off. I'd totally forgotten about how I left the house. The frost had bitten my exposed shins down to onion skin. Weird white spots dotted my legs like the dots of fat in ground beef. My toes were so numb it felt like they were coming off in the boots.

All I could find on Google were photos of famine walls from Ireland, movie stills from *2001: A Space Odyssey*, or big vertical rock formations like Devils Tower in Wyoming, but nothing like I saw out there in the woods. Which gave me more of a reason to photograph it.

What kept me from going was the chance that it wouldn't be there when I looked for it. It had the same dread-inducing feel as the noises in the condo or everything with Itza. Weird, but not totally weird. Not enough to call it supernatural. Benign enough for me to believe I was overreacting.

And if I walked back into the forest and it was gone, then what? I was supposed to attach some meaning to that? Fall down a rabbit hole of clues and mystery and leave you behind? It couldn't have been more than ten minutes we were out there, but it was ten minutes where you weren't on my mind, and the guilt made my throat close. If the wall was there then it would always be there. If it wasn't, I wasn't going to chase down an explanation.

It meant sooner or later I was going to lose you again. No matter how deformed I felt, or how hobbled I was by your absence, with time I would develop the right callus to get on with life and you would slip into the background like a hand on someone's leg that they feel less and less the longer it stays there.

The thought of you wouldn't hurt as much as it did now, and I wasn't sure I wanted that. Your parents buried your body and my brain would bury your imprint on my life. I'd rather hole up in the cabin until the trial, the wall, the world forgot about me.

"Like it out there?" your mom said.

"It's pretty. Quiet."

"They lay the marker down on Vera's grave tomorrow. I'll send you a picture. Or you can just fly out."

With my free hand I was holding on to an old shirt I had rolled up and knotted for Brimley to play with.

"Don't do that," I said.

"Do what?"

"Say I can fly back."

"You can. Many times over with that life insurance money."

"Is that what this is about, money?"

She started to say something but stopped. "I don't want to fight with you too."

The bereavement time at her job was about to run out. Monday she had to go back to work.

"I'm not ready."

I wasn't anyone to tell her she needed to get back on the horse. But she was just as bad as the day you died four months ago, and it was putting a strain on her marriage, her friendships, her work life.

"The networks are calling again," she said. "I told them to get fucked. That fucking piece of shit is filing for asylum because his uncle ripped off the cartel where he's from, and if they send him back he's dead. I hope they do all that *Narcos* stuff to him. Pull his face off and stuff it in his mouth for all I care."

"Offer still stands," I said. "You could come out, visit, get away from all that."

"I might. Maybe a weekend."

Brimley's paws were sliding on the tiles as I pulled the shirt, him scooting backward to tug harder. "I've got a buddy for you to meet."

"Oh yeah?" she said, unsure.

"Jesus, Diane. Not a woman. I found a dog out here."

"Oh." But even that didn't relax the tilt in her voice. Just taking another living thing into my life was too much. Forget telling her about the wall in the forest.

As your mom went on about some issue with the sod over your grave—"They're not watering it enough. I already called the front office because they'll need to re-sod it"—I pictured you standing before the wall, to see how you would go about solving it.

It had been three days since I first saw it, and the wall stayed on my mind. It appeared in my dreams. I was standing on a jetty at the edge of the ocean, and at the end of the jetty was the wall, the sun setting behind it.

After we hung up I started the oven, threw in a frozen pizza without waiting for it to reach the right preheat temperature.

It was snowing outside. Big, cornflake-size snowflakes.

Brimley tugged the shirt loose from my hand and bounced victorious into the living room, curling on the floor and gnawing on the knots. I stared out the back doors, drinking straight from a bottle of whiskey.

In the woods, surrounded by mountains, I could have watched it snow forever. Maybe it had to do with not having to shovel. We measured snow by the inches in the city. From where I stood behind the patio doors, the snow just fell without stopping, but without adding up to anything either.

Brimley nosed his cold snout against my leg, knocking me out of my trance. I hadn't fed him. "Fuck." Luckily I found a can opener in one of the drawers. A spam-colored cylindrical mass slurped out of the can and into his bowl. He ate, drank some water, and went back to his shirt/rope, putting one end in his mouth and walking back to me, pushing his toy against my thigh, looking up to see if I was getting the hint. Those big cow eyes.

I already loved him, and it hurt so bad to love something with you gone because you couldn't experience this love with me. How, if Brimley thought I was okay, he would have *loved* you.

He looked up from his toy again, released it from his mouth. I crouched down against the glass doors, the cold glass running up my spine, and just started weeping. I heard his nails tap on the tiles, then felt his whiskers glide over my cheek and down my face to sniff my tears, his orca tongue licking my face as fast as I was crying, sped up now because he was fitting himself into my lap, all ninety pounds of him, and it broke me.

Whatever, here he was, and you were gone, and he wasn't coy about resting his fire hydrant head against my chest, licking the tears off my chin. He wasn't embarrassed and didn't mince words.

I wondered if he thought, *I want to cuddle.* Or if he just felt the absence of warmth and weight around him and sought to rid himself of the feeling. Like it could have been me or a heated water bag.

His life depended on me, and if I got it wrong he would suffer. And just that, the possibility that something could go wrong, was enough for me to check in with the vet and see if anyone had called for him.

"Already driving you nuts?" Dr. Jacobson said.

"No, not that. More like he's triggering an existential crisis for me."

"I'm gonna guess you don't have kids then."

We'd had a scare maybe a year ago. Two and a half months late. You dipped out of a meeting early and texted me from the women's restroom. *Got my period!* We were both relieved. Before that, we had visited your old boss after she gave birth to her first kid. This was before they diagnosed her with postpartum depression. We watched her putter around the house like an old lady with dementia, looking for the remote even after I'd found it between the couch cushions, tears running down her face. "The master remote," she kept muttering, "the master remote . . ."

It freaked you out. The car ride home was quiet. Neither of us dared turn on the radio. "I don't know if I want it that bad," you finally said.

I'd be a single dad now.

"I can barely take care of myself," I said, mustering a laugh to soften it. It was totally lost on the vet.

"No bite records yet. You can always take him to the pound. They won't put him down right away."

"I'll pass." I rubbed the top of Brimley's head and he arched back.

"You'll get the hang of it," Dr. Jacobson said. "Every existential crisis I ever had ended with a hangover. One must imagine Brimley happy, as Camus would say."

I cut the conversation short after the smoke detectors went off. The pizza was a charred Frisbee I ended up throwing into the woods, a free meal for whatever was out there.

I bought some chicken wire to fence out a backyard so Brimley could run around off leash. Nothing fancy, just a deterrent to keep him from sprinting into the woods again. If he leaned against it the whole thing would probably tip over, but I didn't think he was smart enough to do that. Hopefully it would hold until I could get a contractor to come out in the spring.

With the chicken wire I bought a long bundle of rope and tied it to Brimley's collar and tied the other end to a deck post, with enough slack for him to roam pretty far out and sniff around. I walked about ninety yards from the house and measured out posts for the fence.

If you were anywhere, and watching me measuring out posts, then you were laughing. No way you ever imagined this. Your husband, a real frontier man.

I marked off the distances with wooden stakes. Up ahead was the mouth of the forest. I counted steps in my head, walking parallel with the trees.

A depression in the snow up ahead stopped me.

It was a dry circle of land with a funny assemblage of rocks. In the middle was a stone that looked like black glass surrounded by smaller, regular rocks. No way the wind could have done this. The rocks were intentionally placed there.

It snowed the other day and not a flake had landed on the bone-dry mound.

I pulled the stone off the mound and turned it over in my hand. It looked like onyx, black and shiny, something cracked off the end of an asteroid. Inside the mound was what looked like a sprinkler head that was shielded by the rocks.

The top of the sprinkler was corroded and rusted. A piece of metal like a hairpin stuck out slightly, pinned to the rest of the sprinkler with an aluminum band.

The real estate agent never mentioned a sprinkler system. I couldn't see why anyone would need something like that out here.

A few feet ahead, where another wooden stake would have gone in the snow, was another rock mound, and beyond that one another mound, sitting on the border of my property and the forest. Brimley was over at one of these mounds, pawing at the rocks until they collapsed and revealed the sprinkler head.

I heard a loud pop, like a firecracker, followed by the hiss of a pressurized valve. Something sprayed out and Brimley's face was covered in a bright orange powder. He shook his head and rubbed his snout in the snow, then fell over. It happened so fast. I was less than forty yards away and when I got to him his eyes were rolled back and red froth was coming out of his mouth. His body thrashed with convulsions. I flipped him on his stomach, frantically wiping the rest of the orange off his face with more snow. I carried him to the car and sped into town, my hand on his stomach to feel his subtle breaths. It couldn't happen this fast. This couldn't be happening. I wanted to pull out the shooting script to my life and point it to the sky. The bad stuff already happened. We were past that part. This was supposed to be the resolution. Brimley couldn't die. He couldn't.

The front desk tech saw me peel into the lot. Dr. Jacobson and two other techs were waiting in the lobby with a stretcher when I carried Brimley in, hurrying past the other pet owners who looked away or gasped at his limp head hanging over my arm, me saying no over and over.

———————

Other techs were in the OR setting up an IV catheter, wheeling over the crash cart, waiting to intubate him. Dr. Jacobson put the electric paddles to Brimley's chest. Once. Twice. Clear. Clear.

"I'm sorry," he said after a while. "He's gone."

Brimley lay on the cold exam table, his eyes closed. He could have been sleeping. I laid my upper body over him and felt the warmth was gone. A stiffness and coldness were seeping in.

Not a week with me, and already . . .

Dr. Jacobson asked me to explain what had happened. I told him how we were outside and I had found this sprinkler behind our house—

Our. Fuck.

And how I was scanning the yard for more rock piles when I heard the pop and Brimley's face was covered in orange dust.

"I suggest you go to the hospital to get yourself checked," Dr. Jacobson said. "I think Brimley triggered a cyanide bomb. The Department of Agriculture used to use them to keep wolves and coyotes from getting close to ranches. It's got a hair trigger that spits sodium powder as soon as it's disturbed."

"I don't live on a farm," I said. "What the fuck was this thing doing out there?"

"Maybe it used to be a farm. It's possible the previous owners had no idea it was even there." I think he could see guilt already pooling on my face. "Hey, this is not your fault. This was a freak accident."

"I should have taken him to the pound."

"He might be dead anyway. At least with you he got to have a real home, and someone who cared about him. He was dead as soon as it hit him. Maybe it would have been you who triggered it, and what would have happened to you?"

There was at least one more out there. I could find out.

"Listen," he said. "If I were you, I would sue the shit out of the federal Bureau of Land Management for not removing this thing when they're the ones who planted them. They were responsible for the removal of these bombs once it stopped being a farm, subsistence or otherwise."

My head hurt. I was tired of getting money in exchange for loved ones.

"What now?" I said.

"We cremate the body."

"Do I get the ashes?"

He looked more pained than I did, like he didn't want to give me more bad news. "I'm sorry, Mr. Alvarez. The company we contract with, they cremate the bodies all at once, so we couldn't give you just your dog's ashes. Out here, we don't have many company options to go with."

I wiped my nose and told him I was taking Brimley back home with me, to bury him. Dr. Jacobson suggested again that I go to the hospital. I told him I would, after, but he didn't seem too convinced, and I wasn't in the mood to strengthen my lies.

At the hardware store I paced the aisles, shovel in one hand, my phone in the other, waiting for a page to load with instructions on how to dig into frozen ground.

"Got an outdoor project?" one of the clerks said, and the muscles in his jaw clenched when he caught sight of my face, how red my eyes must have been. I let the tears fall, not bothering to wipe my nose either.

"The dog?" he said, his voice shaved off a level. "You're the one that stray followed around, right?"

Talking, trying to make words, it would have undone me, then and there. Air was passing through the protein fibers that were keeping me together, like the seams were coming apart. I couldn't open my mouth and hoped a nod would be enough for him not to probe the subject anymore.

The clerk cleared his throat. "You're gonna need a cart."

He left and came back with the cart and a different shovel, one with a point at the end. I followed him through the store as he threw in a bag of rock salt, charcoal, matches, lighter fluid, a tarp, two pieces of sheet metal, and heat-proof gloves. He rang up the cost and went over the steps I would need to follow like he was sharing a recipe. I was

still holding the shovel I had picked out. He told me I
could leave it on the counter, and I did, grateful for the direction. He could have directed me back to Chicago and
I would have gone.

"Got any creeks near you? Lake, rivers?"

"Forest," I said.

"Don't bury near the house. You could call the gas
company and they'd mark out your lines. Might take a day
or two."

I shook my head.

"Closer to the forest, the better."

"Wait," I said, lifting my head. "You guys carry potted
trees by any chance?"

The only thing I went inside the house for was the whiskey.

Whatever size Brimley was, the hole had to be bigger
to fit him, then another six inches cleared after that.

I shoveled the snow off the spot I chose, laid the rock
salt, and spread the charcoal over that.

The lighter fluid squirted in thick arcs.

I set the whiskey behind me in the snow and lit a match,
tossed it onto the coals. The fire spread across the ground
and blazed high above the snow. It looked like a trap door
to hell.

Smoke carried into the trees. The heat tightened my
face. When the flames lowered I put the sheet metal over
the coals to trap in the heat.

It didn't feel like hours, which was what the clerk said it'd take for the ground to soften. I just took another pull of whiskey, and another, and another, and with my eyes turned up I saw the sky was darkening into the deep end of a swimming pool. When I knocked my head back again and nothing came out, I tossed the empty bottle and stabbed the shovel into the ground and felt the soil give around its head.

I had peeled both sheets off with the heat-proof gloves and got a weird sense of relief from tossing them off the coals and listening to them melt into the snow. Ash kicked off the gray coals and into the air. The coals broke apart against the shovel, embers floating up, snapping at my eyes. I pushed them to the side and started digging, all that soil going onto the tarp so it wouldn't mix with any snow.

What kept me going was the thought of waking up in the morning to find the grave dug open and coyotes fighting over Brimley's remains, parts of him discarded along a trail that led into the forest. I pushed through the exhaustion. The inside layer of my clothes was soaked in sweat. The shovel plunged into soil that was as soft as coffee grounds.

I ripped open the black bag and pulled Brimley's stiff body into the hole. It felt wrong to bury him in a black heavy-duty bag. It wasn't his fault he was too big for a box coffin. Instead I slid him into a burlap sack the hardware store sold for dried leaves.

He looked asleep, the same way he looked when he

wedged himself between my legs and rested his head on my lap.

I climbed out and poured the dirt over him. With maybe a foot left to fill, I planted a small pine tree I bought from a nearby nursery. This tree would grow and its roots would reach Brimley's body and recycle him. The burial you wanted. It still didn't soften the blow of standing before another grave.

I was so exhausted I crawled onto the air mattress still wearing my muddy clothes, shoe prints trailing me from the back door onto the carpet. Sleep fell over me like an avalanche.

By the time I woke up it was the dead part of night. A breeze was running off my neck. The patio doors had somehow flung wide open.

Outside it was snowing again. I got up to close the door. My hand was on the handle and there, framed in the doorway, was the wall, its corners and face gleaming in the moonlight.

It was standing in the middle of the clearing, halfway between the cabin and the first line of trees to the forest. It was standing at the head of Brimley's grave like a tombstone.

So it could move?

It could sense me somehow, if it was able to find me here, and it took everything in me not to slam the doors shut and hide in the upstairs bathroom. I was uneasy, my insides writhing, and I couldn't escape the feeling. It reminded me of being a kid and getting caught in a lie. How the adult eyes loomed over me, the walls closing in, options snuffed out. No no this was wrong, it was impossible.

I closed the doors but kept staring at the wall, waiting for something to happen. I wasn't sure what.

The treeling was dead. In the wall's shadow it had withered and turned brown. The only part of it still standing was its main stalk. Its needles laid on the snow. The branches had wilted and hung off the stalk like dead skin. Dead. Brimley.

The last half of the day flooded back to me. The cyanide bomb, the defibrillator paddles, the trapdoor to hell, the digging, the burial. Now the wall loomed over his grave. It was claiming Brimley for itself the way everyone had claimed you. My life was a series of disasters, and the aftermaths only attracted scavengers who picked the rubble for parts they could use for their own means.

Maybe because the whiskey was still coursing through me, it put blinders on my attention. All I could think about was destroying the wall. Not grabbing my phone, taking photos, hitting record. Not to document this thing, whatever it was. This wall that could move, disappear, and reappear. That seemed to know what it was doing, choosing to stand on Brimley's grave. For all I knew it was only me and him who'd seen this thing, and he was dead now.

It took a second to strap on my boots, throw on my coat, which was still heavy with sweat and melted snow. One pocket was weighed down by the bottle of lighter fluid. I stepped out into the cold air. The mountains beyond the forest looked more severe. The starry sky sharpened their edges. The whole world was quiet except for my boots trudging through the snow, the wall towering as I got closer.

I pulled the lighter fluid out of my pocket and sprayed down the wall. The fluid clung to the moss, dripping down the ridges of the imperfect slab. I squeezed the bottle until the nozzle spat air.

The whole bed of matches ripped from the package easily. One swipe, a quick scratch of friction, and then a world of fire in my hand, that world smearing space with its arc of light as it flew end over end.

First a blue halo spread across the surface, then all at once the fire was everywhere, flames rising off the wall, crawling up to the sky, the heat pushing me back.

I walked backward until my heels touched the first step of the wooden patio, and then I turned and hurried inside, closing the French doors behind me. I grabbed the truck keys off the kitchen counter and exited through the front door this time and got into the truck. The ignition skipped and immediately turned over. I shifted into drive and the tires crunched through the snow as I drove around the house. It seemed pointless to switch on the headlights when straight ahead was a wall of fire lighting the way.

My foot laid into the gas. The engine roared, frame jerking into a sprint. I didn't care what this would do to me. All that mattered was the wall going down. The amorphous body of flames filled the windshield, the fire giving way to blinding light, a rush of heat.

Before impact I closed my eyes and put a slight bend in my elbows so I wouldn't break both arms.

When it felt like the truck should have smashed into the wall by now I opened my eyes. Smoke was climbing over the windshield, stripping away just in time for me to see I was barreling toward the forest. I slammed on the brakes and the back end fishtailed, bringing the driver's-side door parallel to the trees. The corner of the flatbed hit first, ricocheting the front to smash head-on with another tree. There was nothing and then flash photography. I felt the spray of the driver's-side window against my face.

For the longest time I just sat there, waiting for the pain in my ear to subside. I slowly sat up, wiped the glass off me. I ran through a body check, flexing and moving all appendages. Everything seemed to be working.

My door was dented but it still opened. I got out. The left corner of the flatbed was crushed, but besides that and the driver's-side door, everything looked fine. It took a couple turns of the key for it to start up again.

By now the wall was gone. There was soot on the snow and around the ground where it stood. Bits of the treeling were everywhere, even in the tire treads. There were the tire tracks over Brimley's grave, but the whole wall had vanished, not even a rock fragment left. It had turned into smoke before I could crash into it.

I parked the truck in front and headed inside. I walked to the back of the house and looked out at the clearing to see if the wall had reappeared, but it was gone. I locked the doors.

The wind was brushing a branch against the house, and the noise slipped into my dreams. That's what I thought at first.

It's a pretty normal thing to have the real world seep into dreams. The ears don't go to sleep, they keep taking in sensory information. Someone dreams about a baby crying like a robot and they wake up to hear the fire alarm going off. I don't know.

I was half asleep, passed out on the air mattress, more snow and mud tracked into the house behind me, and the scratching against the windowpane found its way into a dream. The scratching actually built the dream itself. Just an angled view of a window, no window that I recognized, and a bare branch rubbing against the pane whenever the wind blew. I didn't even have a body in the dream. All that existed was the window and the branch, and I had no urge to look away, to doubt its validity.

I woke up to the real scratching noise that was coming

from the back of the house. I rolled over, looked at the French doors. Standing outside was Brimley, pawing at the glass.

"I don't understand," Dr. Jacobson said.

Brimley was leaning against the doctor's legs, looking up to be petted.

"He was standing outside my door this morning."

"This can't be Brimley," he said.

"I know it can't."

"So it isn't."

"Except look at his coat. The way he's acting. That's even his collar. I didn't put it on him."

Dr. Jacobson crouched to scratch Brimley's back, and the dog filled his chest. He scanned him and found no chip.

He stood up suddenly, shifting gears. "How do I know you found this dog outside your door?"

"You're saying I went out and found another Saint Bernard around Brimley's age with the *same* color pattern? For what? To convince you of what?"

"You could want me to confirm your delusion. Since I'm a doctor you think my collusion will make it real."

"I don't believe it either!" I said. "I'm not saying this is the same dog. I'm saying what the fuck is this? What's going on?"

Dr. Jacobson lifted his glasses and rubbed his eyes. He sighed like he was willing to go along with the charade a little longer.

"Correlation does not equal causation, Mr. Alvarez. Did you check the grave?"

"What? No, the soil was still the way I left it."

"If you check the grave, you will find a body. That should prove at the very least that this is not the literal second coming of your dog."

What would me telling him about the wall prove? Second-Brimley was already more than he was willing to humor. He thought I was trying to pull something over him, or that I was having a mental break from reality.

"I can do a blood test," he said. "See if his panels match up with the ones we have on Brimley, but that still wouldn't mean anything. Brimley is dead, Mr. Alvarez. This dog looks like Brimley, but it ain't him. It just can't be. Jesus didn't even come back whole. This," and he pointed to the floor, at the Saint Bernard rolled on his back, waiting for belly rubs, "I don't know what this is, but I would advise you to take this one to the sheriff's office. You'll convince yourself he's yours if you don't. And I don't want to think about what else you'll have to trick yourself into thinking to keep the charade going."

I locked Brimley in the house and grabbed the shovel. His droopy face pushed against the doors, fogging the panes, drool smearing the glass as his eyes followed me. There were no paw prints that led out of the grave to the patio. The only tracks were the tire tracks that ended in a pretzel-shaped trench a few feet away, pieces of fiberglass turning over in the breeze. Brimley was still watching me, his tail wagging.

The digging went slower than the first time. The muscles in my back boiled from the pace. I started taking softer stabs at the dirt once I reached a certain depth, partly afraid I was going to hit Brimley's body and hack off a piece of him. But I didn't want to *not* find his body either, except the soil loosened around the shovel with no sign of the burlap sack holding his body. I was almost sure, judging by where my waist sat in relation to the surface, that I had dug farther than the first time.

Brimley was staring at me through the French doors, sitting perfectly upright, his broad tail sweeping the tile behind him, watching whatever it was I was doing.

Eventually the shovel hit frozen ground again. Maybe I had dug in the wrong spot. Maybe somehow I confused this bare ground as Brimley's grave, when really this was where I turned over the sheet metal off the coals and its retained heat melted the snow all the way to the ground. Except the pieces of sheet metal were still there, sitting on either side of the grave. But maybe the wind blew them over. Maybe my truck never peeled to the side and pinballed to a stop. Maybe the smoke cleared too late and I drove head-on into a tree, crashed through the windshield, my upper body splayed on the hood, and this was the fever dream of a dying brain.

I watched him eat out of his bowl. We sat on the couch and he nuzzled against my shoulder like he used to, which got me to lift my arm so he could dip under it and lie against my ribs, his front paws in my lap, before he slid down and his head rested on my thigh.

How was this not the same dog? I tried to wring out a plausible reason, something that didn't involve the wall or reincarnation or some kind of power or presence to it all. He let me pet him, bunch his tufts of skin together, turning over to let me rub his belly. I couldn't find the bald spot on his leg where the tech had shaved his fur for the catheter. His jowls were white and perfect and without the tinge of orange.

The only thing I was sure of was that I didn't know what any of it fucking meant.

Of course, I knew what I *wanted* it to mean. That pull toward meaning coursed through me.

It tormented me after you died, the urge to look into the past for clues, this *call* behind everything, to draw meaning from it after the fact, to shuffle it into a larger worldview. To make sense of it. Interpret, interpret, interpret. I was at it again.

———

I couldn't eat, couldn't sleep.

I tried reading to calm myself and take my mind off things. My leg started to tingle from the weight of this impossible dog cuddling on top of me.

The book I had pulled off the shelf turned out to be a crime novel, a detective on the cover pressed against a building, a woman in red standing in the middle of an empty street. A torn piece of paper stuck out of the top, more than halfway through the book, but that seemed as good a place as any to start.

She had omen written all over her face. Her smile was as reassuring as a toilet bowl of bloody piss. Her silky hair hung off the chair as she stared daggers through me, exhaling smoke rings.

"What do you want?" I demanded.

"It's really quite simple," she said, waving her cigarette. "Pull me out of the wall. Pull me out of the wall."

The text stopped there, halfway down the left page. The whole right page was blank. I turned to the next page and there was only a single sentence.

Pull me out of the wall.

I flipped again and both pages were covered in blocks of text that read *Pull me out of the wall Pull me out of the wall Pull me out of the wall Pull me out of the wall Pull me out of the wall . . .*

The book fell out of my hands. Its spine clapped against the tile in front of the fireplace and Brimley jerked awake, barking and searching for the source. Adrenaline rushed to my brain so fast that for a split second my vision blacked out—and then returned with tiny black spots floating in the air. I was breathing heavy. Brimley climbed off the couch and I was suddenly standing. The book lay open on the floor like a body, facedown. Part of me waited for it to move.

And without thinking about it, I heard myself say your name. "Vera?"

The house was quiet. Brimley climbed back onto the couch. He gave me a look like I should just ignore it and sit back down with him. I went over to pick up the book when out of my peripheral I saw another book sliding to the edge of the shelf. I caught sight of the book as it fell and hit the carpet. Brimley popped off the couch and started barking again, a higher pitch threaded into it this time, like he was anxious. I reached for that book instead. Not knowing the rules to this, I opened the book to a random page.

Thiago Thiago Thiago Thiago repeated through the entire book.

It was you. I fell to my knees, pitched forward, and threw up.

In grade school an older kid told us a story about a spoiled boy who never listened to his elders. One day he showed his mom a single white hair growing out of his stomach, and she told him not to pull it, but he didn't listen and pulled, and what it ended up being was a very important nerve, and all at once he went blind and pissed himself and lost all control of his body. That's what writhing on the floor felt like. I was undone. You were there, with me, and everything I thought I knew was wrong. I was weeping so hard on the floor that Brimley stayed on the couch and yelped along with my guttural, hominid noises, too scared to even lick the puke I'd convulsed onto the carpet.

This wasn't possible. That was all I could think. This wasn't possible. And still.

"How?" I said, on my knees, facing the fireplace and the bookshelves like an altar. "I don't understand. What is this? I miss you so much. Where are you?"

Inching off the shelf was a hardcover. It crept over the edge and fell in front of the fireplace. I opened it where the spine bent.

Flux Flux Flux Flux Flux covered the pages.

My whole body was seething. I took deep breaths, calmed myself so I didn't totally sprint into the break with reality I might have been having. I needed to think. The bookshelf seemed to be doing the same, waiting.

I pulled out my phone and snapped a photo of the *Flux* pages, picked up the other book filled with my name and snapped those, the far book with *Pull me out of the wall*. I called Diane just to have someone to talk to, to hear me voice all this in case I was incoherent. Maybe she could tell me my words were slurring, she couldn't understand me, and I'd look in the mirror and see half my face melting off my skull in atrophy, the beginning of a stroke. But her cell phone just rang. Her voice mail wasn't set up.

Enough time passed for me to feel like my voice wouldn't splinter as soon as I spoke.

"If it's really you," I said, eyes cast down, "then you know how crazy this is. I need proof. That this is you. Not . . . something else. I need more."

The room went quiet again except for the pops from the fire, then the hiss of four books from the shelf on the left side of the mantel sliding forward, falling off the edge and slamming on the floor, Brimley's hackles raised as he growled. I ran over and grabbed the first book.

18th 18th 18th 18th . . . The street we lived on.

Another book. *Diane Diane Diane Diane . . .*

Benny's Benny's Benny's Benny's . . . Where we always got pizza.

The last book: *Pull me out of the wall Pull me out of the wall Pull me out of the wall Pull me out of the wall . . .*

The maddening part of the last few months wasn't that you were dead, but that you hadn't been obliterated from the world. I could still sense you. The days were watermarked with your face. Your absence felt less like nonexistence and more like we were both in the same house but in separate rooms, cut off by the flimsiest door. The lock on the door was a riddle, and if I could just figure it out, sequence the right thoughts together, you could come back. And here it was. The thing I could do. Pull you out of the wall. As impossible as this was. Illogical.

You were dead.

You were back.

I could bring you back.

The wall appeared after I buried Brimley and the next morning he was alive and wagging his tail outside the door. But I didn't pull him out. I put him in. Unless death itself was the wall, *The* wall. Death cut you off from me, and maybe these slabs of stone held together by mud, this wall, was your threshold to come back.

At the same time I was reasoning all this I was bent over my suitcase on the floor, ripping through the neatly folded clothes. I kept blinking hard, expecting to wake up, at the same time turning my shirts inside out.

The messages split me in half, Vera, and the halves had their own thoughts about what was going on. I was dreaming, I was going insane, I was communicating with you, I was being tricked. The part of me still struggling with what was happening picked himself off the floor and watched the other me still on his knees, rifling through clothes.

Both halves collapsed into each other when I turned a shirt inside out, and stuck along the hem was a strand of your curly black hair. I pulled it out of the shirt and the curls wound around my finger. Brimley stopped whining. He climbed off the couch and sat in front of the glass doors like he wanted to go out. The way he cocked his head, it was impossible not to think that he was mulling something in his head too, arranging the pieces in his mind.

I walked around the couch toward him. His massive head turned and I looked out. Standing in the middle of the clearing was the wall.

I opened the door and trekked through the snow, Brimley bouncing around me. The sun was behind the mountains, giving the snow an arctic-blue tinge. The forest beyond the wall looked black, impenetrable.

The wall cast a shadow on the snow, and it was there the ground yawned open, the roar of soil and snow cascading into a widening and lengthening hole, a deep brown orifice, a new grave, within seconds. A grave for your strand of hair.

How was I so lucky? Humans have tried overcoming death for thousands of years, and I was going to be the one to figure it all out? You were that powerful now? Whatever mechanism was in place to keep the worlds separate, you'd hacked it? We could both hack it? How would I explain this?

Every local station and twenty-four-hour news channel covered your story. We couldn't go back to our old lives. Forget the media, *scientists* would want to study you. Religions. This would change everything.

A few feet before the wall I tasted copper, the inside of my cheeks going raw from sucking in a chunk and biting down until the skin broke, the last thing I could think of to try to wake myself up. The wind and the snow drew out whatever alcohol was left in my system in heavy clouds of breath. This couldn't be happening. Or at least, this wasn't allowed, the dead communicating with the living. The dead coming back to life.

I could think of another kind of story that followed this logic. The kind of logic a person couldn't normally share with someone until they got to know them, so the person wouldn't think they were crazy when they told it. Where messages, weird noises, the dead coming back, weren't easily ignored. Where dead was better. And what was possible, what was logical, didn't matter in this kind of story. Only that it did happen, was happening, whether you believed it or not.

The single strand of hair was around my finger. So many times I watched you straighten it, complain about curls that ran in your family. I ran my hand through these curls when you had a headache. One of the last physical threads of you, proof you were ever really here, and it was clinging to me.

"I need more," I said, looking up at the wall and the dirt holding it together, the web of moss and soil and the glistening stones. "I need . . ."

Brimley started barking. His body stiffened, eyes focused on something beyond the wall. I shifted to see what it was.

Nestled between the trees, on the edge of the forest,

was a staircase. There was snow on the ground and concrete leading up to metal steps, five or six, that led to a blinding event horizon. Framing the steps were subway tiled walls that came in from the sides and followed the steps up to a platform that seemed to be beyond the disk of light. I caught something moving at the far-left end of the field.

It was you.

You in the beige trench coat, arm weighed down by a pastel-green purse, walking through the clearing and into the forest. Your hair bouncing around your face. Earbuds in your ears, no doubt listening to a podcast about finance.

I slipped, running across the field, pushing my way through the brittle branches until I cut you off.

"Oh my God I can't believe it's—"

I spread my arms to hug you and I closed on empty space. I turned around and you were on the other side of me, heading toward the steps. I caught up with you and tried grabbing your shoulder but it was like gripping fog. This wasn't really you. It was some memory, some projection the wall had tapped into and replayed. I walked alongside you, choking on air. It was too much to take in, your face, your gait, like you were blown up ten times too big, an image that was zoomed in too close to make sense of. I could barely avoid the trees, the exposed roots catching my feet, to comprehend more than your lips, your thumb on the phone screen, the curtain of hair just over one eye.

The sound of squealing train brakes hissed out of the event horizon. "Fuck," you said, and hurried.

I realized what this was.

I reached the stairs first and waved them off like the projection would dissipate, but the whole stage kept its shape. I tried pushing you away and fell through you, still not getting it, getting it but not wanting to get it, falling on my hands and knees in the snow. I turned back in time to watch you climb the steps and disappear into the disk of light.

A second later and a shadow pooled on the ground, a small shape that grew wider and grew darker and

I tried catching you but you fell through me.

I was dripping with snow, overwhelmed with grief, the pang of your absence pulsing through me. The steps were gone, a dark and endless forest in its place.

It made sense for this to be the final push. Proof of how I failed you. Of my guilt, my helplessness. Enough to get me to push away my doubt, to do just about anything to keep you from sending me more visions of your death. What better way to get me to pull you out of the wall than to remind me of all the pain I had caused.

That's how I knew it wasn't you.

For the first time out there, I felt the cold enter my bones. Snow in my boots again. The shock was wearing off and I started to shiver. My teeth chattered. I suddenly felt alone out there in the woods, the wall waiting for me in the field, stoic.

Thanks to the snow and my sweat, your strand of hair was glued to my skin. I peeled it off and put it in my mouth, balled it with my tongue into a mass of hair and saliva and swallowed.

I lowered my head and walked out of the woods, into the weak dusk light. The wind cut across the clearing, sweeping the loose snow against dunes that would grow larger before it was all over. The wall was to the left of me. From the corner of my eye I could make out Brimley. He was standing next to the open grave and watched me as I walked back to the cabin.

I had just passed him when a low growl rumbled out of him. It was almost cute. Not the sound—he growled like the devil's pickup truck when it idles—but that I had never heard it before, and it was sort of impressive, that he could lay his head in my lap and lick my face and have this sound inside him the whole time. My big guy.

I looked back and the hair on his spine had risen into a Mohawk. All of his weight seemed to shift into his neck and shoulders, and his whole frame jumped when he jutted his head and bared his fangs, making me flinch.

I put my hands up like this was an arrest, because I didn't know what else to do.

"Easy, big guy," I said. His head lowered, eyes locked. "It's me."

But it wasn't Brimley. His lips peeled back into his ears almost, a zipped-open face of fangs. Gone were those sad cow eyes, replaced with serrated white globules. I stepped back and he snapped at air.

He lunged forward and I bought it, backpedaled blindly as he charged and leaped. My forearm shot across my face. The full compression of his jaws sank into my flesh. I felt the familiar jerk of his head from when we played with the shirt/rope, only now I felt it in my bones. The force of his tugs dislodged random memories, images. Trying to wring a branch off a tree as a kid. The term *socket wrench*.

With my forearm in his mouth, he pulled me toward the wall. When I tried to free my arm, his big head thrashed back and forth and my knees buckled. If I didn't go with the pull it felt like my arm would rip off.

I stepped on something hard and under my boot was the handle to the shovel. With my free hand, I picked it up by the neck and stabbed Brimley in the face with its pointed metal head.

The flesh above his left eye peeled back and steam rose out, red pouring over white fur. I nicked a jowl off. Half of his left ear hung on by a strand of pink. I jabbed the shovel into his eye and fluid burst around the metal. That stunned him enough that he let go of my forearm and thrashed his head, eye gelatin swinging onto the snow.

I ran into the house and slammed the door behind me, expecting it to bang against his head as he tried to push his way in, but he was still where I left him. The whole left side of his face was exposed and blood was pouring over the rows of clenched teeth. He had a permanent snarl there, the rest of his face all hacked up and oozing.

I ran my arm under the cold tap water. The sink filled with blood. His teeth punctures were as round as my wedding band, some of the punctures with a little white peeking at the bottom, some with bright pink walls.

I wrapped a shirt around my arm, spittle shooting between my clenched teeth as I tied it off.

Brimley was standing outside the patio doors now. A brownish gel oozed out of his eye socket and dripped off the side of his snout, firming into viscous droplets on the deck.

We were both breathing heavy, mimicking the same rhythm.

"Go," I said, barely enough force in my voice. I waved my good arm toward the forest. "Get out of here."

Another book slid off the shelf.

It thudded onto the carpet then split open, pages facing down. I backed toward it, the whole time with my eyes on Brimley, this *Not*-Brimley, whatever. Not looking, my hand felt the spine spread on the floor and I picked up the book, turned it over to the facing blank pages. Blank except for a single sentence.

I'm sorry, Dave. I'm afraid I can't do that.

The shirt around my forearm was soaked in blood, running down my wrist and dripping on the floor. All I felt at first was a searing pain around the bite wounds, skin deep, but now the whole arm was starting to throb. Meanwhile the glass pane fogged around Brimley's torn snout as he tracked my movements. I wanted to believe the Brimley I found in the parking lot, he was real, and whatever had puppeted the Itza was pulling the strings of this Not-Brimley, this nothing dog. I wanted to believe that at some point my buddy had existed.

I went for a new shirt in the living room and the dog turned its whole body to watch me, his entire body parallel with the doors, to make up for the exploded eye he couldn't see out of anymore. I watched him struggle to see me as I crouched in front of the suitcase. This meant he couldn't see me grab the keys off the floor and put them in my pocket.

The truck was a straight shot out the front door.

Another book slid off the shelf and landed next to me.

"I don't care," I said.

Not-Brimley pushed his face against the doors to see me grab the air mattress and drag it closer, his blood and fluid smearing the glass. The few feet to the door left me out of breath, dragging it with one hand. I was going weightless in my toes, fingertips. It hit me that I might pass out before I could get out.

One side of the mattress rested on my thighs, its other end pressed against the bottom of the door like a slash mark.

Not-Brimley's tail started wagging as my good hand reached for the handle.

One quick turn, enough for the latch to free itself from the frame, and Brimley's growl was inside the house. I kneed the mattress off me and turned and ran, hoping it would push the door closed once Brimley was inside, and I could reach the front door and close it behind me and trap him in the house.

I ran down the hall like a monster was chasing me. I ran so hard I lost all feeling in my arms and legs, like if the knob didn't turn I would just run through the front door. I could hear the plastic of the mattress rub against the floor, then the sound of panting, his weight striding behind me. I got to the door and half expected the dog to crash into me, but when I opened it and just as fast slammed it shut, in that small window of the door closing behind me, I saw he had already calculated he wouldn't make it and was doubling back to run out the patio doors.

Whatever this was, it pretended to be you. Convincingly. I nearly gave over a piece of you. So I wasn't sure if your mom, waving from the passenger seat of a Lyft as the car approached the cabin, was part of its doing. I was losing blood and still I had to stop and stare at her.

The expression on her face went from joy to confusion to extreme terror. She slapped her hands on the windshield frantically and pointed to something beyond me. The dog had rounded the cabin and was running me down.

I didn't think I could make it to their car. The driver slammed on either the gas or the brakes and got the car stuck in the snow. I gunned it to my truck, the doors unlocked, because who needed to lock their doors in such a secluded place? I slid across the front seat and reached back for the door and closed it on Brimley's massive head, his jaws striking up at my outstretched arm. The steel frame ripped the flesh off his skull as he pushed his way into the cabin. Thick bacon strips hung off the sides, slobber and blood whipping onto the seats, the dashboard.

I felt a rush of air behind me. Diane was standing on the other side of the truck with the passenger door open.

"Get the fuck out!" she said.

I pulled on the driver door as hard as I could, turning my body so my feet were closer to the passenger side before letting the door go. Brimley climbed in and I spilled out the other side. Diane slammed the passenger door shut as the dog barreled against it. I scrambled around the front grille and shut the other door, locking him inside.

Diane threw my good arm over her shoulder and kept me upright as we staggered to the Lyft car. The driver was on his phone, rambling into the receiver about a man being attacked by a dog.

We scrambled into the back seat. I looked out the window as the driver sped off, rounding the bend of the road, past the field and the edge of the forest. I could see the dog calm in the truck, watching me watch him, the space between us growing wider and wider.

III.

Your mom swore we talked the whole way to the hospital. She kept asking me questions to make sure I didn't pass out. She said the only time I lost consciousness was when they doped me to clean the wound.

I don't remember any of it.

For me, what happened was that I watched the cabin and my truck get smaller and smaller, the night gathering around the house and its few lit windows until they looked like embers in an empty fireplace and the darkness snuffed them out.

What happened next was I felt the spray of something cold on my face. The roar of waves crashing into rocks drew closer, louder.

I opened my eyes. Diane, the car, the snowy mountains, all of it was gone. The chill in Colorado softened into a warm breeze. I was lying on a small piece of beach made mostly of pebbles and pastel-colored shells. In front of me was the ocean and a clear, Virgin Mary–blue sky stretched above it. The waves crashed against a row of jagged teeth on the edge of this little stepping-stone of land, attached to the base of a ninety-degree rock face no way I was going to try to climb.

On the left side of the beach, the jagged teeth of stones grew bigger and continued into the ocean. They were big slabs of black rock stacked on top of each other to create a jetty stretching almost half a mile into the water, waves crashing against the old stones, white froth washing over the surfaces. At the very end of the jetty, like Rose standing on the bow of the *Titanic*, was the wall.

"You shouldn't be here."

I recognized the voice. At the other end of the beach was the cook with his back to me, but he wasn't wearing his white apron and paper hat. He wore dark canvas pants rolled halfway up his muscular calves and a dingy tunic. A villager out of an Aesop fable. I never paid attention to his hair because of the hat. At the diner, his gray hair was cropped close on the sides, but now it had grown, hanging halfway down his back like a wet mop framing his Frankenstein head.

He stood on the edge of the landmass, barefoot, where the pebbles and shells gave way to larger, sharper stones. I could see he was looking into the dark water, where the tide crashed against the shore.

"You shouldn't be here," he said again, but he didn't

sound mad. And this time I caught a strange accent in his voice but couldn't place it. "Nothing's ready yet."

I brushed the sand off me and walked to where he was. He was staring at something poking out of the water. The waves and white froth crashed around the object in the water, but when the waves settled, you could see a stone ring sticking a couple inches out of the surface. The ring was part of a larger structure, maybe a well, but how deep it went was lost in the shimmer of the water. I looked into the ring and saw shapes darting back and forth in the dark pool. Fish.

"It's to starve them," he said, "keeping them trapped like this." He turned to me like he wanted to gauge my reaction. On either side of his mouth were deep crevices that lengthened his face, making him look like a half-starved ghost. Those webby, bulbous eyes. The eyes of someone choked to death.

"I'm dreaming," I said.

He kept on about the fish. The trick was to starve them for a week, sometimes longer, to remove any off-flavor from the flesh.

"For what?" I said.

He gazed up and looked out on the ocean, his mind somewhere else. "For what I've been preparing for you," he said. "The banquet."

"What banquet?"

The waves crashed and the noise was deafening.

"What do you think of this island?" he said. "This is

better than the mountains, yes? The flora and fauna are plentiful. You won't be bothered by another soul."

The warmth, the ocean spray, were intoxicating. I felt stoned. I kept squeezing my eyes shut and opening them again, pushing my fingernails into my palm, anything to wake me up. Because I could feel something else laced in the warmth and pleasing smells, a metallic aftertaste that coated my mouth and continued down my throat, absorbing into my blood. Becoming a part of me, crawling up my spinal cord like moss. A thought, a longing. How easy it felt here to let go, not hold on so tight. It took everything to lift my arm and point to the other end of the beach, where the jetty cut into the ocean and the wall stood at the precipice. "And that?"

He blocked the sun from his eyes to see where I was pointing. "Oh, that. It's just an interface. You've got so many boundaries around you. You were born with them." He walked over to me, his hands clasped behind his back, the wind in his hair. "So many barriers, defenses. For us to get to know each other, there needs to be a threshold. Do you love the island? They're all here."

"Who is?"

"Everyone you've ever loved. Your family. The dog. Her. The earth is not a good place. It's slippery. You live on the edge of a blade. On one side is an abyss. On the other side is an abyss. Whatever happens on the blade, the horrors, I can't control." He sounded pained at this. The sacs of fluid under his eyes drooped and revealed pink flesh brimming with tears, the way a sick dog looks, the way an ill-fitting mask would sit on a person's face. "It's better here. White sand and water as far as the eye can see. Couldn't you just be here forever?"

He brought his hand to his mouth and sipped from a chocolate shake that looked similar to the one he made for me. The red straw darkened, the veins in his throat flexed.

He swallowed. "Last time we met, I gave you something and you were eager to pay. We were standing on a chessboard. Another interface. Have you forgotten how the pieces were? I haven't."

"Why are you doing this?" I said, the words a jumble in my mouth because my tongue was numb.

"Grief has inured you to dumb questions." His voice flickered with agitation. He went back to staring into the ring, where the fish darted and swam and plunged and rose again. "The shape was drawn in your home. The flesh was flayed. It can't be taken back."

I felt my edges dissolving, at the same time being drawn closer to the stone ring. The fish swam and swam, looking for food, hungry, dying, and he would kill them, and they would never know the point of it all. That it was for our benefit. Our hunger, our palates. All they would know was the pain.

I woke up in a hospital gown not unlike the one you wore. My view from the bed, propped up with a pillow and your mom sitting next to the railing, watching me, it was the same view you'd have had if the coma broke. What a mind fuck. Diane spent days waiting for you to open your eyes, praying, and it ended up being me who woke up.

"How you feeling?" she said, and in typical Diane fashion she didn't wait for me to answer. "They irrigated your arm out. It was gross. You'll need rehab but the doctor said you'll be all right."

From the elbow down my arm was wrapped in a gauze bandage. What they did was called debriding the wound. The doctor cleaned the area and with a scalpel, forceps, and scissors, he cut away dead tissue and washed out the punctures, measuring the bite marks and going half an inch wider with his incisions, the way I dug Brimley's grave bigger than his body. The urge to read into this picked at me and I pushed it down. Not everything had to mean something. I was suddenly exhausted.

It was dark outside the second-floor window. I had been out for a few hours. The sheriffs stopped by earlier to talk to me and talked with Diane instead.

"They shot the dog," she said.

"Good." My throat felt like an exhaust pipe.

"What happened to him being this great dog? I thought you liked him?"

In the span of a few hours my body had withered and contracted. The muscle on my arms looked stiff, twisted over bone. My joints were dried out, ash in the sockets, and when I moved it felt like a mortar and pestle breaking down gunpowder.

The words collected on the other side of my teeth. The urge to tell her filled my throat, except I knew if I started talking the whole thread would undo me. And where would it start, with an apology? For being the one to wake up in the hospital bed instead of you?

"You okay?"

The tension spread behind my face, like a fist pushing through my sinuses. The words pushing through concrete.

"There's this . . . this thing . . ."

A familiar trail of warm tears fell down my face.

"I thought it was Vera . . . It might have . . . killed . . ."

"You're not making any sense."

Then a pipe or something burst, whatever mechanism was in charge of shuffling the words in order for the sentences to come out with meaning, and it spilled all at once. "Last night, or whatever night it was, the night before you showed up, I started getting messages . . . in the book I was reading . . . like direct messages, with my name, your name . . . repeated over and over . . . impossible . . . it's how the dog came back, the dog died the day before and I buried him . . . the one you saw was a second one, like a bad copy—"

I could hear how incoherent this all was but couldn't stop myself. It kept pouring out, the wall in the woods, the cyanide bomb, how maybe the wall put it there, or maybe

Brimley had always been the wall, a stream of word salad Diane's face showed she couldn't follow, and I couldn't stop. ". . . to pull her out of the wall . . . the stairwell in the woods and she ran through me . . ."

Tears running from my cheeks down the tubes. How this all started with an Itza we used to own.

Before the verbal mudslide could finish she sat back and pretended to watch the mounted TV. She patted my hand as I kept going, like she was tapping out. She looked to the door, willing someone to walk in and see me babbling and maybe stick me with something to calm me down. The tears started down her own cheeks, her choking between breaths to say, "Stop, stop . . . ," barely a whisper.

And just as soft, I couldn't stop saying, "I'm sorry, I'm sorry . . ."

The discharge instructions went over how to dress the wounds and change the bandaging. The doctor handed Diane prescriptions for pain meds and antibiotics to be filled.

"You'll need lots of rest," the doctor said. "And you'll have to take care of this dog situation."

"Sheriffs already took care of that, doc," I said, and your mom wheeled me to the elevators.

I had Diane call Dr. Jacobson's office to see if the sheriffs had brought Brimley's body to his clinic. I wanted to tell him by all means, burn this one. But the office was closed.

Diane guided me through a packed lobby filled with slumped-over people, crying children.

"Where to?" she said.

"A hotel."

"The dog's not there anymore, Thiago."

"I know that." As soon as we were outside I got out of the wheelchair. Cabs were idling in the turnaround and I waved one over. "I already told you. I know how it sounds, but this isn't the drugs, or grief. It's not some coping mechanism. Something's out there. Something's following me. And I don't know what it wants."

It was hard to read her by the expression on her face. She either felt sorry for me or annoyed.

"We'll get a hotel then." She didn't sound convinced of anything. This was her placating a scared child, allowing me to go on with this. She wasn't buying anything supernatural, or at least she wasn't admitting to it. We both looked out at the mountains like what I was talking about would crawl over the peaks and descend onto the town, limb over limb.

The cab pulled up and she sat in the front. "I want you to take us to the fanciest hotel in town. It's on him."

The way to the hotel took us past Dr. Jacobson's office. A string of patrol cars and sheriff's cruisers were parked in front. Red and blue lights swung over the heads of people milling outside the front entrance, holding their dog leashes and cat carriers. A wide circle was cordoned around the door with police tape.

I told the driver to stop and we pulled over. I asked them to wait for me, except Diane got out too, telling the driver to yeah, wait for us.

We crossed the street and joined the other pet owners. A man with a collie said there'd been an accident, the whole place needed to be evacuated. Anyone boarding their pet in the clinic got a call from the police to show up now or drive out to the shelter.

Someone else said it was a break-in, and the police didn't stop to correct anyone.

The front desk tech stepped outside and rocked back on her heels when she saw me. Her bloodless face triggered a sudden wave of anxiety.

"Mr. Alvarez," she said. A sheriff passed by her and she stopped him, said something in his ear, now both of them staring at me. The sheriff looked at the gauze wrapped around my forearm.

He waved at me to cross the yellow tape and I did. Your mom hung back. The tech and I walked into the clinic's waiting room, which looked exactly how it did the last time I was there, except instead of owners and their animals it was filled with sheriffs and police, flashes from photos being taken in other rooms, the static of radios going off all around us.

And the smell. It was unlike anything I'd ever smelled in my life. Right away I started gagging, taking a second to gather myself. The tech stepped away and came back with a surgical mask for me to wear. For a vet clinic to smell like piss or shit was one thing, but this was not one of those smells. This was something spoiled. The six-month-old package of ground beef in the back of the fridge with all the blood pooled at the bottom. A cracked sewage line or septic tank. A stench that festered in the creases of something huge and menacing.

The sheriff asked if I had been in contact with Dr. Jacobson since yesterday. I told him the last time I talked to Dr. Jacobson was when he saw my resurrected dog. Of course I just said "my dog." Then he asked about my arm and I told him what had happened. My dog bit me.

"Does this have something to do with me?" I said.

He opened his mouth but the tech cut him off. "Dr. Jacobson is missing." She was a mess. "The sheriff's office called him because they had your dog, and he met them at the office so he could receive the body. We have to perform a postmortem on any dog that might have rabies. Dr. Jacobson's wife called me when he didn't come home. I came back to the office and—I found—I found your dog, the one that the sheriffs put down. In the exam room . . . I'm very sorry to say this, Mr. Alvarez. The room is covered in your dog's remains."

"What do you mean, 'covered'?" I looked over to the hallway of doors that led to the exam rooms. Light pooled out of one of them into the hall. All kinds of people in uniforms and protective gear filing in and out.

I asked if I could see and the sheriff said it was an active crime scene still. He said the walls, the floor, it was all covered in a kind of substance, originating from the dog's corpse but still unknown as to how it achieved its pattern, which looked like an explosion. The chest cavity of the dog was exposed and limbs were hacked off, placed in some odd pattern. He said someone from the sheriff's office would contact me about retrieving the remains when they could be made available to me. My own chest was pried open and filled with ice.

"No one loved animals as much as Dr. Jacobson did," the tech said, and cried. "This was sick. Whoever it was who did it."

When we got to the hotel, the people at the front desk checked us into a suite. Diane and I took the elevator to the third floor without saying a word. We were both tired. The drugs they gave me at the hospital were starting to wear off. My arm ached, and Diane's downcast eyes kept shifting left to right like she was trying to read the floor for some kind of answer, but I was happy to have her there with me. The doors opened and she waved for me to go first. "Age before beauty."

"Would you believe me if I said I missed you?"

She chuckled. "Just keep it moving."

The bellboy was waiting at our door and set Diane's luggage inside the room. I tipped him while she ordered room service. I fell asleep to the sound of her flipping through the channels. My dreams were rushed together, anxious. One where I was floating in black space. Another where mummified corpses sat around a dining table and their hands were folded in prayer. Another dream where I was falling. My shirt collar was damp with sweat when I woke up.

Diane was sitting in her bed and drinking one of those little liquor bottles from the fridge.

"Those are like twenty bucks a pop," I said.

"Really? Hey thanks, Thiago."

She had her shoes off but kept her coat on. A western was playing on TV. She looked transfixed, the way she brought the tiny bottle to her mouth and back down again automatically. The whole time her eyes stayed on the grainy shoot-out surrounded by mountains, smoke spilling out of six-shooters and men clutching their guts. It was that same look she had at the wake, between the times people came up to hug her, snapping her out of the thousand-yard stare, overlooking a field only she could see.

Diane gave us the hardest time when we first started dating. Your stepdad was way easier, this quiet guy who went about his husband and father duties without complaint. The way he showed people he loved them was by finishing their basement or changing their brakes. It took maybe two visits for him to set a beer down in front of me and ask me to help him break down some old furniture for the firepit. "He likes you," you said on the car ride home.

Diane didn't warm up so fast. She worked in a packaging warehouse on an assembly line, and even though most of the jobbers there had been with the warehouse for twenty, thirty years, there was always a revolving door of young guys who would get hired on temporarily. Guys her daughter's age but without a college degree, who had no ambition, no sense of urgency to their lives, spending all their time out with friends, their clothes stale with weed stink, and she just knew the stress they had to be putting on their parents, on any woman who was dumb enough to mate with them.

Crabs at the bottom of the barrel. Her nightmare coming true in me.

She once asked where I pictured myself in ten years and I said reading a book with a dog in my lap.

"Where are the kids?"

"With their parents?" Such a smart-ass response was a reflex, and a nervous laughter trickled out of me to fill up the void her stoic face generated. You looked at me from across the table like I had missed all top-five answers on the board before you busted out laughing.

Diane knew you didn't need a man to take care of you. That wasn't her problem with me. Her thing was that I didn't measure up. What she wanted was a man who would be equal to you, on your level.

Her job let out early because her shift started at five in

the morning. I never told you this, but I took a day off to wait in the parking lot until they let out, older folks in orange shirts and stained jeans, paint-flecked boots from other jobs. Your mom pulled off her safety vest as she walked over to me.

"What's wrong?" she said.

"What? Nothing." I realized how it must have looked for me to be standing out there, my face no doubt pale from what I was there to say. I told her I had already talked to your stepdad. I was there to ask her if I could propose to you. She folded her vest and then folded it again, squinting like the sun was in her eyes, except it was overcast.

"If I say no, then what?" Her voice was a duck in a pond, calm on the surface and chaos under the words. I didn't know what to say, so I settled on the truth. "I'd probably ask her anyway."

"Why are you here then?"

"To be polite?"

"She's not a little girl anymore," Diane said, looking off to nod goodbye to someone. "She's grown enough to live with her mistakes."

That woman was sitting with me in a hotel room a thousand miles from home. Her daughter was dead and she was drinking because she couldn't sleep, watching over her daughter's husband. She finished the tiny bottle and cracked another one open. "Back at your place, when we were driving off and the road climbed out of that valley, and we could see from above . . . What was that thing, behind your house?"

My heart kicked awake. The blurriness in my eyes cleared from the adrenaline. But I didn't want to say it. I didn't want to put a word to it and harness what she saw into a shape. "What thing?"

"That . . ." And she broke away from the tractor beam the TV had on her, looking down at her lap. "It was like a statue or something. One of them Stonehenge-looking things." For the first time ever, she was looking at me like she was in need of something I could provide. Context. An answer.

"First time I saw it," I said after a long pause, "it wasn't behind my house. It was in the woods. Brimley ran off and I chased after him and that thing was out there between the trees. Then Brimley died and I buried him in the clearing, and that night I saw the wall again in front of his grave."

As she worked out what I was telling her, her eyes scanned left to right like she was reading a book I couldn't see, and conflicting emotions divided her face. Confusion in her forehead, sense of absurdity along her mouth, eyes set to suspicion.

"I don't know what it is, Diane. That same night I drove my truck at it and it turned to smoke. That was why my truck was busted up. I went through it and hit a tree."

"That was your dog in the truck," she said, trying to set me straight, or get the story in line. "He was attacking you."

"That wasn't him—and I know how crazy that sounds. The vet could tell you. He saw Brimley when I first brought him in. He saw his body after a cyanide bomb that is supposed to keep wolves away went off in his face. And he saw that second dog that showed up outside my door, the one that looked exactly like Brimley, right down to his collar. Maybe it reanimates the body, like it needs a vessel."

"What does?"

"The wall."

"Jesus, Thiago. What am I supposed to say to this?"

"Nothing. I'm not telling you to believe something even I don't believe. I'm just telling you what's happening. You saw the wall, the dog attacking me. The vet's missing now. His exam room apparently looks like a Thanksgiving turkey exploded all over the walls. It's on the tip of my tongue, the thing I want to call this, what's happening, but it's too crazy, it's not real. It showed me Vera." I said that last part quickly, forcing it out.

She turned to me with exhaustion and disgust. I was including her daughter in my mental breakdown.

"Books started falling off the shelves with messages inside," I said. "It tried to convince me it was Vera. Like Vera was talking to me through the books and telling me to pull her out of the wall. It gave me your name, where we lived. Believe me, I wanted it to be Vera. Her hair's still caught in my clothes, I figured I could bury a strand and it would bring her back like it did the dog."

"Then why didn't you?" she said accusingly, and the water in her voice betrayed how angry the tone was, her lips quivering.

"I guess I needed more convincing, so out in the woods it showed me the day she died. It re-created the platform right between the trees. I saw her running to the stairs because she didn't want to miss the train . . ." My voice was flaking away. "I saw her go up those stairs and fall, and I knew it wasn't Vera. I knew, if she had a chance to talk to me, if this was our one chance to see each other again, she wouldn't have shown me that. She wouldn't have used her death to convince me. Ever. The wall figured out it made a mistake and sicced the dog on me. That's what you saw. I think it followed me here. There were things happening in the condo before Vera died, little things we couldn't explain. Random music being played, lights, messages on the fridge, the Itza. It would—"

"Vera told me," she said. "The thing was malfunctioning, right? Responding when no one said anything."

"Buying stuff on its own. Swords and acid and all kinds of weird shit."

"She told me about the dildo."

"Oh, yeah. That too."

A caution crept over me, like a blanket being pulled up to my nose. I couldn't be sure she wasn't the wall. Would Diane fly out to see me without letting me know? Well, yeah. She would do it just to see if she could catch me with another woman, already moved on. She used to show up to the condo on weekends unannounced with two pounds of carnitas and horchata and talk to us while the bed creases were still in our faces.

"I'm not expecting you to believe me right off the bat."

"I'm from Mexico, Thiago," she said, drinking the small liquor bottle. Her parents brought her over the border when she was six. "I'm sure you've got family from over there who've told you stories. Everyone's grandpa has met the Llorona, everyone knows someone who can heal with their hands, everyone's got a tía who can see spirits and talk to the dead. I'm sure little Thiago laid awake at night because he thought he heard the Cucuy in his room."

The darkness in our room deepened with the name Cucuy. She was right. When I was little, if the light wasn't on in a room I had to run in and flip the switch while talking out loud, because somehow light and noise kept the Cucuy away. Because there was no real shape to him unless it was in the dark, and the longer you stayed in it the more real he became.

She was sitting cross-legged on the bed, rocking slightly. Diane never seemed her age, and now she looked, not younger, but just as clueless as I was. I think I wanted her to assume the leader role, to be the mom, the way I'd seen her so many times when she stopped by and started picking up after us and needling you over little things. I needed that person to point me in the right direction, to call me stupid or ignorant for even entertaining the idea of the supernatural.

"It's proof," she finally said. "Of an afterlife. Vera's somewhere else. She's not dead." She stopped to let the rush of emotions pass, released them with a long, cool exhale. "She's not dead," she said again.

I didn't want to point out that this thing, whatever it was, was trying to make its way here, to our world. Maybe what was on the other side was worse.

But I was done with knowing things, figuring things out. I just wanted to lie next to you and talk about nothing. Every mystery screamed to be solved. The wall, Brimley, the falling books, my dreams. And I needed to make sense of them, trace a story out of the strangeness. One thing meaning another. The same way people reduced you to something they could buy to remember you. Something standing in for something else. Interpret, interpret, interpret. I lay back down, sick of the circles being run in my head. I looked up and saw patterns in the ceiling panels.

Something grabbed my shoulder and I was sure I was dead.

"Thiago," Diane whispered.

The television was off. She was crouched in the space between the beds, holding my shoulder like she had been shaking me for a while.

She put a finger to her mouth, and that was when I

heard it. I pulled the blanket off me and slowly sat up, try-ing not to make the bedsprings creak. A clicking sound.

Light from the hallway seeped around our room door. I could see two blots of shadow in the light filling the space between the door and the carpet. Feet.

Something higher caught my eyes and I followed the movement. The door handle slowly turned and stopped on the lock, the clicking noise. Someone was standing on the other side of that door.

I took your mom's hand off my shoulder and got out of bed. The feet on the other side of the door shifted slightly. They turned the knob again. Whoever was outside gently pushed on the door to see if it would open. The carpet sounded like TV static under my bare feet.

It could be another hotel guest thinking this was their room, drunk and confused.

Diane cradled the phone off its dock and dialed the three-digit extension to the front desk.

"Hello," she whispered, her hand cupped around her mouth and the receiver. "We're in 326. Someone's trying to get into our room, please help."

I shuffled one foot toward the door, and when it didn't make a noise, I moved my other foot forward.

"Thiago," Diane whispered behind me.

I looked at her and put a finger over my mouth.

The peephole was the only other thing giving off light. The feet shadows were perfectly framed so that if I looked through the hole, the person's face would be right there. Almost like the person was waiting for me to see. They wanted me to see. I had crept another couple steps forward when I heard the elevators open down the hall. The doorknob stopped turning and the feet shadows swiveled away.

"Sir?" I could hear a voice calling from down the hall. "Excuse me, sir?"

I ran to the peephole, looked through. There was no one.

The concierge passed our door as he followed the person, telling them to stop. Two security guards arrived outside, looking in the direction of the concierge. I opened the door. The concierge was walking back toward us, talking into his radio. He notified all staff that there was a trespasser in the building and for everyone to monitor the exits, stop anyone suspicious trying to leave.

His eyes followed a trail of something dark as he walked toward us, the trail stopping in front of our door. It looked like mud. Mud and something else.

The only other room available that late at night was a honeymoon suite the hotel staff personally escorted us to, me and your mom holding our things with sleep still in our faces like roused kids being pulled out of the car. But he could still be hiding in the hotel somewhere, even though the concierge doubted it. Since the halls were considered common areas, no trespassing had actually taken place, so there wasn't much more the hotel could do about the unidentified person. The hotel felt contaminated with his presence. We decided to move to a different hotel two blocks down and slept on firm mattresses, cigarette smoke caught in the room's drapes.

Like either of us could sleep, though. Diane flipped through the channels, sipping on bottled water because there was no mini-fridge. The television light blanketed us in the dark room.

"I want you to fly back," I finally said. "As soon as possible."

"Why?"

"This thing won't stop. I don't want anything bad to happen to you too."

"So how do you plan on stopping this thing on your own?"

I didn't know. I couldn't stop it but maybe I could take myself out of it. Stop running from it.

All those orders that were delivered to our home. How convenient it'd be now to have a rope and pull it around my neck. Sit in a bathtub full of water and inhale a rag soaked with chloroform. It couldn't keep chasing me if I was already dead.

Your mom could see it on my face. "You think killing yourself will stop it?"

"It might."

"Well that's not happening. Vera would kill you for killing yourself. Just stop and think for a second. If all this started at some point, that means it can end too. You said it all started with the speaker thing. Then what?"

"It might have," I said. "I don't know. We heard scratching in the walls first. She said I was crying in my sleep."

"What did you do with the Itza?"

"I ran over it." And the shame rolled over me because maybe this thing grew in power because I released it. But that would also mean it lived in the Itza. So it could split open the ground and make the dead rise but couldn't bust out of hard plastic? Somewhere in a factory a window was open and an evil spirit floated in, got too close to the assembly line and was trapped in a glossy orb five inches tall?

Diane rolled her legs off the bed to face me. "What about the bruja?"

"The who?"

"Vera told me about the tenant who used to live there. Someone sacrificed a goat or something on a pentagram. Vera said you were trying to track the woman down."

"It wasn't a pentagram," I said. "And the animal was skinned too. The real estate agent couldn't tell what it was."

"Whatever happened? Did you find her?"

Blood receded from my fingers and toes, and in the dark room a chill crept over me. Fidelia's doll eyes rose to the forefront of my mind. "I did."

She urged me to go on with her hands. "And?"

A different kind of shame rolled over me. A familiar one. "She only spoke Spanish. It was hard for me to understand what she was saying."

Diane's mouth hung wide open in what I thought was disbelief. *Here we go*, I thought. The what-kind-of-Mexican-are-you speech I'd heard my whole life. My heart jumped when instead of letting me have it, she fell backward on the mattress in a fit of laughter.

"What? What is it?"

She was holding her sides, rocking left to right. "Oh my God, Thiago. What if she told you how to get rid of this thing but you no ha-bles es-pa-ñol?"

"Hey," I said, sitting upright in bed. I could feel myself fighting the infectiousness of her laughter, but my voice was already tuned with levity. "This is serious."

She wiped her eyes, the last few chuckles working themselves out of her. "Oh God, that felt good."

"Vera never told you I can't speak Spanish?"

She sat back up. "She never had to. I've heard you order food before."

It felt good to smile. "Yeah, Vera was the Spanish speaker in our house. I wish she went with me to confront that old lady, but at the same time I'm glad she didn't. The woman admitted to killing the thing and drawing the shape on the wall. I think she did it to get revenge on the new owners for kicking her out."

"What did she draw on the wall?"

"This like, giant rectangle, I guess. About the same size as the wall that kept appearing at the cabin."

"Maybe they're connected."

"She said something about Canal, like Canal Street,

but I couldn't figure out what she meant. I ended up driving up and down Canal Street for almost ten miles, but I didn't see anything."

"Are you sure she meant 'Canal' and not *canal*? Canal in Spanish means channel. What if she meant a passageway, or an opening."

"A portal," I said.

She tapped the back of her hand against the open palm of her other hand as she talked, momentum building in her voice. I was glad to see her spring back to life, but I was still stuck on wishing this would all go away. "Okay, so . . . Let me think for a second. What if the wall in the clearing is the rectangle she drew in your condo? She called this thing into the world, to your home, but the only way for it to enter is for someone to pull it out. For some reason it wants you to do it."

I tried to say something against this. Portals? Sacrifices? But all I did was push air out of my mouth, words failing me.

Diane grabbed her phone and put the call out to her family members and anyone else she knew who believed in the supernatural and had dealt with evil spirits. Christ. It was enough to make me laugh if I wasn't so scared, hearing her recall the past few days like someone talking to their doctor about when they first noticed their symptoms. Those people put the call out to others, a friend waking her grandmother for advice, a cousin in Mexico riding his motorcycle into the badlands to visit a brujo to see what he could offer.

She finished the last call and rested the phone on her chest, waiting a second before she talked to me. "We have to go back."

"To Chicago?"

"To the cabin. It's where it was strongest, where you saw the wall, the dead dog, where it showed you Vera and communed with you. It's there you banish it."

"I'm a fucking wizard now?"

"They gave me instructions. There's got to be a store we can—"

"I'm done, Diane. I'm sick of all this. I'm sick of being alive without her. I don't care anymore. About anything, about going on. For what? What do I have? And don't say 'us.' Don't say I have friends and family who love me. I'm not going to live for their sake. I'm tired. More tired than I've ever been. It's in my bones. I don't want to keep going. I don't want to see how this plays out."

"Listen dummy, if Vera—"

"Vera's not here," I said, louder, one foot off the bed. "She never could have imagined this would happen. And I want to see her."

"What if that's what it wants? What if it does all this to make you give yourself up? You don't know if suicide will stop it. You might kill yourself and fall into its hands. Vera wanted you to *live*. She made sure you'd never have to worry about money so you could live your life. She didn't leave a fucking gun for you with one bullet in the chamber. I can't stop you from doing anything, Thiago. I don't know why this is happening to you. But whatever this is, whatever's behind it, it wants *you*. So don't let it win. You're already hurting. You're already in pain. So quitting won't stop it. Let's get people to believe you. Or let's kill this thing. You don't want it to hurt anyone else. So we go back to your place. We wait for it to come back. That way it sticks with us."

I could hear you in her voice. I could now see the influence Diane really had over you. How Sarah Connor begat Sarah Connor.

My only condition was that I do this alone. She couldn't take part. She just couldn't. And she nodded solemnly.

The cell phone rang. It was your stepdad. A family friend had called their house instead of calling Diane back on the cell. He wanted to know what time zone was she in that she was making calls this late, and what did she need to know about banishing rituals for? Her excuse was impressive: she wanted to bless the cabin before she left, the way her mom did for their home, and they never had any problems with evil spirits, did they?

She did the whole *yeah-uh-huh-okay* routine that signaled the end of a conversation, and after their *I love you*s but before their *talk to you later*s she said she would be home in two days.

I pictured you laughing. *Yeah Thiago, my mom's totally going to listen to you.*

I guess whatever problems your parents were having after your death, they were at least on speaking terms now. It reminded me of the times we went to bed with whatever it was we were fighting about still unsettled, and even if it was me who started it, you still got into bed and rolled over and bopped me on the mouth with your tense, puckered lips. "I love you," you'd say, like words could push someone if you said them hard enough.

Diane's decision to stay sank to the bottom of my stomach, and I had no fight in me to push it out. I relented. "Have you ever had problems with evil spirits?"

She laid the phone back down on her chest and reclined against the pillow. "I already told you, Thiago. I'm from Mexico. We're all a little haunted."

A Lyft driver took us to the cabin and pulled in next to my truck. The passenger door was left open, and we saw the dried blood and white stains of slobber strung on the seats and the dashboard. The window was webbed with cracks, the glass broken around a central point where the dog had been smashing his head against the window. I tried not to think about it. We unloaded our things from the car and the driver turned back around, heading for the main road.

It was getting dark, orange behind the mountains. A

strong breeze rolled through the woodland, the rustling branches and twigs sending us into a panic, whipping around and searching the tree line for anything that would pop out and attack us. We had the shot nerves of nine-year-olds after they watched a scary movie. The orange dusk only made the landscape stranger.

I walked into the cabin first, holding my bandaged arm out like it was armor. Diane carried the shopping bags and dragged her suitcase because she refused to let me carry anything.

We'd spent all the daylight shopping. Diane wrote a list of supplies during our continental breakfast in the morning. We took car after car around town, gathering the specific herbs and tools we'd need.

I was already regretting this. Coming back here felt like we were returning to the scene of a crime. All that Mac-Gyvering for me to get away and now we were giving it another chance to catch us.

The wind funneled through the living room and front hallway, turning the dark and empty rooms into caves. The French doors at the back of the house were blown wide open. The whole place felt like the discarded husk of an insect. We kept our coats on because we weren't sure if we'd have to run back out right away.

Diane switched on the flashlight app on her phone and we searched the house. I closed the back door and locked it. Outside the trees looked like charred pillars. The field behind the house was empty, snow over the patch of land where the wall had stood and the ground opened into a hole.

We flicked on every light in every room. The books were still facedown on the floor like dead bodies. Diane picked one up and flipped through the pages that were now filled with their original story, chapters, and dialogue. Nothing about a wall.

"This is a nice place," she said, assembling the bouquet of herbs she was going to burn so she could carry the smoke all through the house. No amount of burning potpourri could make me want to stay there, but what I was going to do with the cabin was the furthest thing from my mind at that point.

I relit the pilot light and the furnace kicked on. Forced air roared all through the rooms.

Supplies we bought to defend ourselves: three canisters of salt, handfuls of sage leaves, anise, amaranth, one pen, one notepad, one white unscented candle, one white ceramic bowl, and two .38 specials.

"Something light," I blurted at the gun store clerk.

"But'll pack a punch too," your mom added.

He showed us a few options and we settled on the Ruger LCRx because I could shoot it fairly decently with just one hand, something the range attendant gave me hell over trying when we practiced at the shooting range.

I cleared a section of snow off the deck and spread a thick white line of salt outside the back doors. Diane poured half a can outside the front door. We took the remaining can and a half and spread rings around the sink drains and bathtub drain in case it could climb out of the pipes.

The salt recommendation came from two different sources with two different reasons. One said the mineral was a byproduct of the ocean and therefore a symbol of the source of all matter and life, reminding the spirit to return to the underlying ocean of eternity. The second said a visiting spirit is compelled to count any spills you purposely make, taking it as a challenge, except since they lack a body they can't move the grains they've counted and will inevitably lose count enough times that the frustration will force them to leave. Which I guess meant even in death there was still forgetfulness, OCD, frustration. Passing away didn't alleviate us from the things that made life so tedious to begin with, we were beholden to that shit even in the afterlife. But whatever. I poured the salt.

Diane was in the living room, sprinkling holy water with her fingertips. The water she poured into her hand was slightly tinged an olive color.

It wasn't the water that originally came in the bottle we bought from the gas station. Diane chugged that water before we walked into the closest church we could find. Expressionless statues from all corners watched as I blocked any view of your mom submerging the bottle into the basin of holy water. The glug of bubbles escaping the bottle stopped and she capped it, backing away the way we came in, under the lifeless eyes of nameless saints and naked angels trapped in stained glass.

We were running down the church steps as Diane held the railing and made the sign of the cross. "Thou shalt not steal," she said, when she saw me looking at her.

"He can see what we're dealing with," I said.

We walked farther down the block to catch another Lyft. While we waited, Diane told me about the time she found a church missal in your bedroom when you were eight years old.

"You're lying," I said.

"Hand to God," she said. "I wasn't even mad. I was just curious why Vera stole it. You know what she said? She was tired of not knowing the words everyone said at mass. She was trying to memorize the responses."

Self-imposed homework? It didn't surprise me one bit. All the times I saw you stress over Yelp reviews before we picked a restaurant for one of our birthdays. You were convinced you could learn Japanese before we ever visited Tokyo because you didn't like the idea of not being able to communicate.

Our Lyft pulled to the curb and we got in. Neither of us talked on the way to the cabin. I was thinking about what Diane said the night before in the hotel. How you wanted me to live. I was sure that if the roles were reversed, you wouldn't have stopped until this thing was dead. You would have pushed Fidelia to fix all this. Brimley wouldn't have had to die. Was that why the alarm never went off? If this presence or whatever could control Itza, make me see things, open the ground like an orifice, then maybe it could already see there was no give in you. No concession. I was the easier mark. It fucked with the alarm and triggered a Rube Goldberg set of circumstances that ended with you dead, and me ripe for the picking.

Diane went to each window in the cabin and wet the sills and ledges with the blessed water, going from room to room and muttering prayers.

Next was the banishing ritual. No one could agree whether we were dealing with a ghost, a poltergeist, or a curse, but they all agreed a banishing ritual needed to happen, outside of me eating certain regional plants and vegetables that weren't on hand at the local grocery stores. But a white candle, a legal-size yellow pad, and a white bowl, those were easy to find.

The first step was a spell. The spell was that I write the big problem out. I was to start from the beginning and focus on the spirit or devil or whatever, and how it had affected my life, our life, in every way, being as precise and specific as possible. Once I had it all down, I'd light the candle, set fire to the pages, drop them in the white bowl, and watch the story burn.

That's what this is. Me trying to get it all down.

"I don't know how to start it."

Diane looked over my shoulder to see how far I'd gotten. "No, no, what about the scratching noises? And your dreams? You have to include everything."

What goes first. What goes where. What connects to this. What means what. Writing's never come easy to me. In grade school I hated book reports, and that hate only grew for high school essays, research papers, group papers.

"You're not doing this for a grade," your mom said. "Just write what's happened. Write it like you're telling Vera."

Write it like I was talking to you, filling you in on everything that's happened since you've been gone. What I've learned about the things that were happening when you were still alive. I ripped a clean page out and put that in the beginning. If I opened my eyes and you were standing in front of me, whether I was dead or dreaming, and I had the chance to talk to you again, what would I say?

Your parents wouldn't let me bury you in a tree pod.

I would go for the joke. A callback only you would get.

The gears in my head turned, a riddle solved.

I wasn't imagining it. I didn't reconstruct it. A real experience from the past played in my head and I *felt* it. You rolling your eyes, fighting a half smirk. You saying, "I know."

Some parts have gotten clearer in the writing of them. Some parts are so frustrating that I feel like a spirit that counts salt. I'll get to a new part and see how stupid I was not to notice what was happening. It's hard not to see how many times we could have stopped this. How you might still be alive.

But other things have gotten clearer, and each time I've sat down with the pad it feels like I'm honing something,

I'm paring something down, I'm that car commercial where the guy stands in front of a block of clay and carves out a new design. And it was the idea of talking to you, that the flames would engulf these pages and the words would roll into the smoke and float through the veil and you would be there for it, that helped me figure out a way to get this all out. Down on paper. Thank you. I love you. I'm sorry. Thank you. I love you.

I'm sorry. For the things that still need to be written out.

Diane walked up to the second floor and into the far bedroom that faced the road. The herbs made a brushing sound in her hand as they lightly bounced against her forearm, zigzagging the smoke trail as it rose before her. Then the brushing noise stopped.

"Thiago."

I stopped writing and headed upstairs into the empty room where she was standing in front of the window looking down at the clearing. The snow had absorbed some of the indigo dying out of the sky as the sun disappeared behind the mountains. The field looked like the top of a glacier, blue-white. The forest deepened in the shadows, and from the window we could see deep tracks in the snow, tracks that exited the forest and doglegged toward the cabin.

Dr. Jacobson was at the front of the tracks, staggering

through the snow. His white coat swept open and the wind rattled its flaps. He was walking with a limp, or like one of his legs was asleep, because it didn't seem painful to him. It looked more like he was trying to get the hang of legs as a concept, trying to sync the hips and knees and feet more fluidly. His arms were stiff, hanging on either side like weights. The horseshoe of gray hair around his shiny bald head was tousled in the breeze.

"Zombie" didn't fit, but it was the only word coming to mind. When he got close enough to the cabin for us to see his face, he stopped.

Diane backpedaled from the window, holding her mouth. "Oh my God."

"It's Dr. Jacobson," I said, staring at him staring at us.

That dog had torn his face apart. Deep trenches of claw marks ripped across his face, the flesh inside almost purple. It almost looked like camouflage, one eye sitting in a pool of blackness. It was Dr. Jacobson but it wasn't the man I'd met in his clinic. There was Dr. Jacobson and there was the abstract thing, the one setting him in motion. Whatever had been lurking in the dog was puppeting him now. I guess. I was making it up as we went along.

He leaned forward, bending stiffly at the waist, and charged through the snow, moving like it was the body that kept him from moving faster. We ran downstairs and checked the doors and switched off the lights so he couldn't see into the cabin. But there was no sound of the knob turning. I looked out over the patio, my breath fogging the glass, but he was gone.

"I'm calling the police," your mom called out, slinking back into the kitchen for her phone. The screen unlocked and she started calling, the silence so pure and the air so thin I could hear the dial tone from across the room.

My eyes were drawn to the light of her phone reflecting off her face. I turned back to the French doors and Dr. Jacobson was standing outside, watching me. I pulled away from the glass and an unconscious groan lurched out of me. Diane's whisper climbed into a shriek as she spun back to see him. She screamed and told the 9-1-1 operator an intruder was trying to get into our house.

His face was the aftermath of some ATV course in the rain. His right eye sat in a bed of black ink like an eel's head poking out of its cave.

The things that were happening in our condo, as long as we never drew them to a single source and gave it a name, it couldn't take shape. But with every strange noise, every random package, it had felt like we were being pushed toward calling it what it was, calling it into existence, and when we did the world would laugh at us. We pretended it didn't exist and you ended up dead. Every unexplained memory was crashing down on me, collapsing into a single source. The condo, the dreams, Itza, the cyanide bomb, the wall, it was all the same thing. *Ghost* didn't feel like a big enough word.

Evil, all-powerful. That was what the cook said. "What if it's not the world, but some other *thing* doing all this to you?"

His bulbous eyes. The creature in the red glow of the brake lights.

A demon.

"Do you see what happens when you make me work?" Dr. Jacobson said. It was not his voice. The words sounded strummed, vocal cords being plucked, not vibrating under their own power. He scanned the doorframe before his eyes switched back to me, then over my shoulder at Diane, who was holding the ax I'd bought to chop wood. She swung the ax head off the ground and hefted it in her hand.

His head moved lazily, weirdly fluid. An invisible tentacle seemed to extend and rest on anything he gazed at, and it cut through the ocean of space to the next object, me. He smiled the way a drop of oil separates in a hot pan. "Claim your seat at the banquet."

"What's that?" Diane said.

His dead gaze shifted to her. "Where Vera resides. Where they all reside, and the sound of their mewling carries to the shore."

"Vera's in heaven," your mom said.

"You will learn to call it that."

Spit and blood flecked the glass. His heavy breathing fogged over it. He was standing there, but the damage Dr. Jacobson's body sustained in the Not-Brimley maul had destroyed this new vehicle. Maybe we could wait for the body to fall apart on its own. He swayed to one side, head lowered in a drunken pose. I almost expected him to fall against the doors.

"Why are you doing this?" I said. For the first time, he noticed the salt in front of the door. "Why did you kill my wife?"

"I didn't kill her," he said, studying the frame again. "You did."

"What? No I didn't. That kid did. You made him."

"You did," he said again, and looked at Diane to gauge if she was listening to him, if it was connecting with her. "To remove distractions."

I was grasping at things I could say that were proof of how I didn't kill you, the thoughts rushing to me so fast that I was stuttering, looking at Diane and feeling desperate. "From what?" I finally said, the only thing that made its way through the threshold of my mouth.

"From the task."

It had been hammered home at this point. To pull him out of the wall.

I could see a shadow moving on the kitchen hardwood, between me and the door. Diane was moving back into the kitchen, where he wouldn't be able to see her even with both eyes, let alone the pit where his left eye used to be.

"Why are you doing this?" I repeated, trying to buy her time.

He rolled his head along the base of his neck, fighting off the rigor mortis in the muscles. "Ya sabes, güey."

It was another voice, the syllables cascading down to a deeper, heavy register, the sound of old boulders rubbing together. It echoed through me. A voice I hadn't heard in a long time. My father.

Dr. Jacobson dropped into a crouch, his right knee collapsing inward as it bent at an impossible angle, with the foot still rooted forward. The exposed nub of bone on his index finger hovered over the grains of salt, and it bobbed as if he were counting. Then his gored face peered up to me, blood seeping through his smile, and he swept the salt away.

His hand gripped the handle and the latch broke as he turned it open. I yelled for Diane to run as I backed away from the doors and slammed against the kitchen island. I turned to follow her out the front door, but she wasn't there, and the door was closed. I looked back to Dr. Jacobson. He stepped into the house and your mom came out of the kitchen shadows with the .38 cocked and extended in her hand, the barrel pressed against his temple. She fired point-blank into his head. The sound was so loud it had body. I felt the boom move through me. I opened my eyes, expecting the doctor's head splattered everywhere.

The force of the gun blast didn't even nudge him. He greeted the bullet with an evil smile as it exploded out of its chamber, but it didn't hit *him*, the doctor, the one standing before us. Even now it's hard to describe. It was like your mother shot into the fabric of existence and created a vacuum. The doctor's head caved in around the small hole where the bullet entered, and the noise emanating from the vacuum sounded like screams, a mass howling. My hands shot over my ears and I watched my lap darken with warm piss, like my body knew what that sound was even if I didn't.

The gun was sucked into the hole with your mom still trying to fire another shot. Her whole hand was yanked into his head. She brought up her knee and anchored it against the doctor's sternum, her other arm locked at the elbow, pushing off his chest while she screamed uncontrollably, her head flailing like hell.

Dr. Jacobson's body was rigid. The hole in his head widened to the size of an airplane window framed by his ears and jaw and hairline. His whole face was gone, drawn into itself. Diane's knee trembled and gave and her body shot forward. It all happened so fast that by the time I ran over to her she was shoulder deep into his head, her feet barely touching the ground, head peeled back as far as she could.

I pulled her by the waist but it only moved her lower half. Through her I could feel the force of the vacuum reeling her into him. Her eyes rolled into her head and white froth spilled from the edges of her mouth. I hooked my arms around her ribs and shoulders and pulled. The white froth dripped onto my forearms. I braced my foot against the doctor's waist and pushed until my legs burned, until

I brought up my second foot on his waist and pulled until my own muscles wrenched into places they weren't supposed to go, constricting around my spine, slipping into sockets.

Diane's jacket sleeve ripped off and disappeared into the black space. Your mom's arm flailed wildly in the vacuum and now it looked atrophied, withered to a mummified limb, except it was slick with a milky, yellowish fluid. As if her muscles had liquified and were oozing through the pores of her skin. We fell to the ground while the doctor's caved-in head looked down on us. Framed by his ears and jaw and hairline was a window to an unknowing darkness, darkness upon the face of the deep, and a vacuum pulling air into its orifice, a ripping noise close to screeching. I grabbed Diane by the armpits and dragged her as fast as I could toward the front door. The doctor didn't chase us. He stood there and his void-face watched us retreat into the hall. I reached behind me and opened the door, pulled your mom onto the front steps and closed the door like that would do anything.

She was barely breathing. Her pupils rolled back and then her lids squeezed shut from the pain. The skin on her arm was still yellow and waxy, dotted with black spots. Some of her fingers were stripped to the bone.

From far off I could see three pairs of headlights driving out of town. They were still a few minutes away. But if we could hide long enough, maybe we would make it out.

I grabbed your mom and dragged her toward the

snow-beaten path that would lead us through the curtain of trees and back onto the main road. The path led into complete darkness. Diane was moaning, trying to talk.

The cabin's front door opened, but the doctor wasn't there, only shadow.

An orange glow covered the snow around us, and I heard the whiff of flames.

The wall was blocking our path, covered in fire.

Those headlights rounding the bend, they were joined by sirens and red and blue lights.

I pulled us away from the blaze and into the trees, where even in the shadows, out of the glow of the raging wall, the sheriffs would be able to see us. Your mom's mouth hung loose, eyes halfway open, the lower halves of her pupils strung out.

"Diane? You've got to stand up. We can run for it."

A white light cut between the trees.

The only thing it could possibly be was the headlights of one of the cruisers. I waved in the direction of the light, trying to get them to see us.

The white glow was stationary, like the cruiser was parked, except I didn't hear an engine idling, and its swirling emergency lights were off too.

I threw myself against trees the closer we got to the light, not wanting to let go of your mom. I pushed off one, slammed against another and leaned against the sharp, cold bark, struggling to catch my breath. We stumbled forward again and the trees gave way to the light.

Instead of headlights, it was Itza. Itza stationed on our white console table.

Her LED hexagons pulsed. Light was cast on the snow and the trees, giving them an alien texture, jagged surfaces with indented spots, the shadows creating the illusion of faces in the trees.

Your mom rolled across my body. I caught her as she turned and her lifeless face stared back at me.

I was leaning against the tree, but I was also standing in front of Itza in my boxers and a T-shirt, standing in the snow. It was a version of me, a projection like the one of you running to catch the train. Standing, hands at my sides, hunched slightly toward the glowing orb, mouth open.

"Itza," I heard myself say. "Cancel alarm."

"You're lying!" I screamed, as if the forest cared.

I heard the air slice, scissors cutting through construction paper, and something slammed into my back. The walls of my lungs touched. I hit the ground and slid forward against the soft layer of dirt and snow.

Dr. Jacobson was standing over me with the shovel. I couldn't breathe, could barely concentrate over the reverberations of pain rippling from my spine. My hands trembled as I tried to crawl away from him. He grabbed my right ankle and dragged me away from the sound of the police cruisers making their way around the bend, the sirens and light bars cutting through the night again. I slapped at the base of the trees in an attempt to stop him from taking me wherever we were going. Snow packed into my nostrils. I looked up again and saw the perimeter of the tree line as it pulled away from me. We were moving farther away from the cabin. I turned over and saw Dr. Jacobson had dragged me back into the clearing, where an open grave was waiting, the wall stationed at the head, doused in fire. A wind kicked the flames higher, the licks snapping out the faint flurries coming down, the flames guttering lower to reveal the surface of the wall as black and slick, mottled like cartilage, its mortar deformed into a malign expression.

My voice was frayed, tattered, when I tried calling for help, that I was over here. Dr. Jacobson stopped at the edge of the grave and threw me in, and the drop was almost worse than the swing on my back. I heard something break in me somewhere, what sounded like furniture snapping into place. The night sky was splattered with stars, framed in the opening of the hole. Then came the dirt, shovels' worth pitched over my head. I closed my eyes, extended my hand out, and the doctor swung the shovel like a golf club and shattered my hand. He jabbed at my head with the point of the shovel, trying to push me back in. The sharp edge opened my scalp, and warm blood poured down my face. My legs were already buried. I could feel the dirt's weight press on me, and in the end, it felt good.

———

The dirt falling into the grave sounded far away. Before the weight got too heavy I curled into a ball to make a pocket of air. It was all I could think to do. Old movies ran through my head of characters waking up in coffins and realizing they needed to calm down to conserve their oxygen. If I kept trying to crawl out he'd hit me with the shovel until I stopped. The mass of soil sat on my ribs, my joints, pressing against my skull like a vise. The little light coming from the stars was snuffed out. I was being crumpled like a piece of paper.

The soil became a black ocean of granules and crystals. I kept shaking, and even though I knew I needed to conserve oxygen, I couldn't calm my stomach from taking in deep breaths and filling this pocket of space with more carbon dioxide. Fear split me into two pieces. One part was a feral animal flailing in a hole out of sheer panic, the other, a disembodied voice locked in a bone cage, trying to soothe the animal enough to get it to listen.

I could hardly hear the shovel anymore. The vise around my head melted away.

All I could feel was the cool dirt. The darkness was still there, but the pressure against my ribs disappeared. Then I was weightless, and the way dirt was passing between my fingers, I thought the ground beneath me had collapsed and I was falling. But I wasn't scared, because dying felt like sinking into a deep, calm sea.

I closed my eyes, ready to let go.

I opened them when a bubble seeped out of my nose.

My head knocked back, swinging the rest of my body so I was floating upright. The world was gone and nothing but empty space surrounded me, but I could see my body, my arms floating. Light was coming from somewhere, so I looked over my head and saw a shimmering white disk. Dark slivers passed over me. From their fins I could tell they were fish.

I swam toward the disk.

The panic returned. The trapped air in my lungs was seizing across my chest, crawling up my throat. Water bubbled all around me. My thrashing created a white haze that made all the fish hide along the walls. Through the disk I could see the wavy shape of the cliffside, of the cloudless sky beyond it. My arms and legs banged against stone bricks that wrapped around me like a sphere. I went from swimming to pushing myself off the walls of the well.

My only focus was getting to the surface and breathing. Not wondering what I was doing in the stone well the cook used to starve fish before they were served. *For the banquet.*

I could see the dark shape of him above the water, looking into the ring. Someone else stood next to him. I was close enough to the surface that I could hear muffled voices, a barrage of voices that didn't match the two calm shapes watching me.

One voice yelled, "Drop your weapon!"

Another one: "Down down down!"

A different voice: "Do it now!"

My fingers clawed between the stones. Bubbles spewing out of the corners of my mouth. I was close.

Something roared over the commands, so violent and heavy that the shapes above heard it and turned. It sounded bigger than a human, bigger than any animal not extinct. Gunshots popped over and over while I kept climbing.

One of the shapes standing on the stone ring bent down and stretched out their hand. I reached out of the water and the shape clasped my wrist, pulled me out, and I gasped for air.

I was halfway out of the grave and next to me lay Dr. Jacobson's body, steam rising out of the puckered holes sprayed across his chest and face, three other officers still with their guns pointed down on him. Their flashlights were clipped to their vests and the beams swung all over the place.

The cop let go of my arm and pulled me by the shoulders, telling me I was safe, asking if they needed to look for anyone else.

IV.

Two detectives stood next to my bed, one on each side, looking down on me. There were no loved ones left to take their place.

I went on the record. Dr. Jacobson attacked us because he was possessed. He was possessed by a wall that had also resurrected my dog, that sent me messages in books, pretending to be my dead wife. What lived inside an Itza had killed my wife. It was after my sanity. It needed me to give up.

Even with Dr. Jacobson's face the way it looked, and the sound he made before the police filled his chest with bullets, they thought I was crazy. I could see it in the way they turned to each other and shared a tense look like this was going to be a waste of time. What choice did they have? They were men with jobs and bills, and wedding bands, their phones probably filled with photos of their kids. Men who worked for their paychecks and held certain beliefs about how the world worked, and their victim was talking movie nonsense.

It was fine, really. As long as I didn't have to hold the pose anymore, pretend the impossible wasn't possible anymore, they could think what they wanted.

They logged everything in the cabin as evidence, even the letter I had written you. Dr. Jacobson was pinned with Diane's murder and his body was never released to his family. Last I heard, Estes Park police had handed the case over to the FBI.

The police called your stepdad to tell him someone attacked Diane and she had died from her injuries. He asked if it was his son-in-law who did it. This rattled whoever called him and they passed this information on to the detectives assigned to the case.

"Why would he ask if it was you?" one of them said.

"Because of how you told him. He knew she was visiting me. Who else would he think?"

They were there in the hospital to drop off some of my belongings from the cabin. The doctors wanted to monitor me because they didn't like how a couple disks looked in my spine. They wanted to evaluate the swelling as it healed. I had a fat black centipede of stitches running the length of my scalp like a part in my hair.

I told them to let me know when your dad arrived because he wasn't answering any of my calls. Everyone went on about how I needed to sleep. An officer sat watch outside my door, bored with the cooking shows that ran constantly because I was too afraid to change the channel. The lights needed to stay on all the time. I needed the curtains drawn, then I needed them open. A nurse injected something into my IV line.

"What is that?" I said.

"It's to help with pain management."

Your stepdad arrived at the hospital, went straight to the morgue to identify Diane, and flew back home with her body without visiting me.

I slept but didn't dream.

When the doctors finally signed the discharge papers, it was an orderly who wheeled me out of the lobby. They put one arm in a cast and removed the stitches out of the other. Days had passed since your dad left. I took a cab straight to the airport and flew standby. Stacked at the news kiosks, instead of Esteban Lopez's face, it was Dr. Jacobson's, and the accounts of his murderous rampage.

I missed the wake but made it in time for the funeral. Held at the same church where Diane held yours. A lot of the same people sat in the same pews, wearing the same funeral outfits. But when people saw me no one smiled. No one extended their arms for an embrace. The word was out. Something was wrong with me, and maybe detectives couldn't draw supernatural conclusions, but these people could. They didn't need to read my statement to know I was damned in some way. The old church ladies would call it El Mal de Ojo, the Evil Eye. Everywhere I went, death and destruction followed. Another mangled branch sprouting on the Alvarez family tree. Two more dead women to hang from it.

The sorrowful embraces from before were now stiff handshakes. Instead of coming over to say hi, your cousins nodded and turned to the person next to them. It looked like it hurt when they smiled.

They gave me a wide berth.

Your stepdad sat in the front pew, flanked by family with more milling in front of him.

"Mr. Diaz," I said, and the half circle of family members parted. He was sitting with his face in his hands and he looked up.

The words dissolved in my mouth.

"I—"

I tried not to picture your mom.

"I'm so sorry—"

The last time I saw her.

"So sorry . . ."

I wanted to pay for Diane's funeral costs. We looked in each other's eyes for a split second and he nodded and I nodded. He grabbed my hand and held it for a long time, like he needed the support or he was finding a way to for-give me in that moment. I hoped it was the former.

The procession stretched for half a mile, my rental bring-ing up the rear. After every intersection we crossed I saw people in other cars raise their arms like *finally*. A random car tailgated me for more than a few blocks, exploiting the free lane traffic gave us. It was almost comforting to be in a city that didn't care, full of people with somewhere else to be. What did it matter to them Diane was dead? Life is life.

Here I was, back at your grave, this time to see your mom be buried next to you. I never got to see the marker Diane bought before I left. The photo she picked to be etched into the marble was from a friend's dinner we went to. I was the one who took the photo. I remember steady-ing my arms against the table because I was drunk, but I liked the way you were leaning, half-drunk yourself. Your arm was holding your head and you were listening to the person across from you tell a story. The punch line to the story came and you closed your eyes and just smiled harder, and I snapped the photo.

We each lit a paper lantern. After the priest said some fi-nal remarks, we let them go, watched them float above us, a parade of lanterns, a marketplace in the sky, ascending out of the Virgin Mary blue and into the deeper, oceanic blue I thought maybe bordered the edge of the world. I couldn't help but think, if Diane was anywhere, if she could see this, she was laughing. She got me to light a candle after all, and stand there with her loved ones and watch the hot air collect under the wax paper to propel the light farther out, feeling the vastness of the sky, its staggering depth, so much to take in that I panicked for a second, worried the mass of blue would crush the paper lanterns, leaving only wisps of smoke left over, the way ocean pressure could crush a submarine. Except as they got smaller and the shapes of the lanterns were all but gone, we could still see the glow, they continued, and surprise surprise, my weeping days weren't over.

Diane's death reminded me that the ground beneath my feet was collapsing into a widening hole. Death was encroaching and nothing would stop it.

I'm afraid that when we die, we end up wherever we always thought we'd end up. If we want to go to heaven, we go to heaven. If we believe in reincarnation, we come back as a baby or an animal or a tree. If we think we're going to hell, we'll burn forever, and we'll never realize that we were the ones to put ourselves there. That in the afterlife we all tapped into a mechanism, some larger system bent on fulfilling our personal ideas of death.

You believed that once a person died the party was

over, so you'd just be sitting in an empty space, in a self-imposed slumber. But then I'd die expecting to find you, spending all my time traversing an afterlife landscape that I make up as I go along, searching, when all I'd want would be to sit in that darkness with you, blind and mute and floating in the ink like a womb.

I'm afraid I'll die wrong. The sperm that swims down the wrong fallopian tube.

I don't want it to be that what I believe is what matters most. I want the truth, without a brain to skew it, without eyes to filter it.

Only a couple of your friends offered their homes to me. They waved me off when I said I was staying at a hotel, but there was no way I was putting anyone else at risk. The doctor was dead, and everything had been quiet since then, but that didn't mean shit. The damage was done. I kept expecting to see the cook everywhere I went, and not seeing him only made my nerves fray and snap even more, my shoulders hunched to my ears, because I knew sooner or later he would come back for me, and then what?

I struggled to string together a few hours of sleep without waking up in a cold panic, scrambling to do something that would convince me whether I was dreaming or not. Looking at the clock helped, because numbers were hard to make out in dreams. I'd stick my arm out and try to will something across the room to float into my hand, and when it didn't, I knew this was real, not that the real followed any kind of logic anymore either. A man with a black hole for a face existed in the real world.

I stayed at a hotel downtown. A nice one. I figured spending my money was the best way I could honor Diane. A hotel with security in the lobby. At night I tried piecing together what this could all mean. This thing wasn't satisfied with killing and reanimating Dr. Jacobson, or Brimley. It only used them as puppets to get to me. The veterinarian was the only one whose death I didn't see. By the shape he was in when he stalked us at the cabin, it couldn't have been an easy possession. The process had torn him to shreds. He was already half dead when he appeared on the patio. Maybe it always made a mess of a body it had to force its way into.

I ordered room service and answered the door in a robe and slippers. I ate in one bed and watched television, got up, and slept in the other bed. Before going to sleep I set my phone against the television and opened the camera, switched it to video, and hit record, to see if I got up at all during the night without knowing. I had started recording myself sleeping after the hospital let me go.

One morning there was a knock on my door. The front desk clerk delivered an envelope marked URGENT.

From the Law Office of Names I Didn't Recognize. It was a letter from a private attorney saying there was a petition to declare me mentally incompetent and have the life insurance money be moved over to your stepdad. The letter said it was on behalf of the Diaz family, but it didn't say who had initiated it. The police report from Diane's death was mentioned as reason for concern. In it was all the ammunition they would need to show my grip on reality was fading fast.

What the Diaz family didn't know was that I had no intention of fighting this. I had no intention of staying in town either, should this go to court.

Before the front desk clerk knocked on my door, I had bought a one-way ticket to Durango, Mexico. It was where my mom grew up. Where you and I spent a weekend in a small town named El Ranchito, just outside of Canelas, after my mom died and I wanted to visit the places she had told me about. Her cousins picked us up from the airport and showed us around. They took us horseback riding. We shot guns in the desert, drank pulque out of an old paint bucket, picked up tarantulas with a shovel and threw them at each other.

"When the world ends," you said, the both of us sitting on a blanket, watching the clouds glide over the expanse, "this would be a pretty cool place to hole up."

I walked to a nearby bank and withdrew the maximum amount of cash I could pull out of the ATM in case a judge froze my account. High-end restaurants and boutiques surrounded the area, but I knew if I walked a few blocks in any direction that stuff fell away. After crossing a main intersection I found a neighborhood sports bar on the corner the roaming hordes of Cubs fans seemed to overlook.

Inside it was musty and tiny particles floated in the beams of light spilling from the windows to the floor. The booths were filled with guys who looked like if you slapped them on the shoulder concrete dust would waft into the air. Their long, somber expressions were pointed at the glass between their hands.

The TV was playing a basketball game no one seemed to care about. Def Leppard played out of the jukebox, but the place had the air of a church.

I perched on a stool and a stocky bartender with a white handlebar mustache set a drink napkin down. I ordered a double bourbon and sat there, turning over Diane's funeral card in my hands.

When he set the bourbon in front of me, the Def Leppard song started to skip. No one turned but me.

The big display window on the jukebox showed an open book filled with songs, and the pages began to turn like someone was standing there and searching for a song. The bartender muttered something under his breath. He ducked under the bar to our side to check out the problem, but as soon as he did the pages stopped flipping. The display lights flashed, followed by the strum of an exaggerated acoustic guitar.

"*Hit it,*" was the first line.

The bartender stared at the jukebox for a beat before

walking back around the bar. Whatever happened with the change in music woke the other drinkers and they shifted in their seats, said something to their neighbors, and lulled themselves back into their long stares.

I think I was the only person actually listening to the song. The glass of neat bourbon felt like an ice cube in my hand.

You may think I don't hear you, and that may make you blue . . . But I got plenty of time, so who you talkin' to . . .

I downed the drink and over-tipped, and left.

A steady flow of cars passed through the street but the sidewalk was deserted. I passed an alley on my left, trying to twist my arm inside the cast. Just that first verse of Itza's song instantly drew a sweat that collected inside the cast and itched without any way to get to it. I could feel the start of a headache rumbling.

From the corner of my eye I saw a shadow. But that wasn't what made me stop. What made me stop was the singing.

I'm here whether you neeeeed me, here whether you seeeee me . . .

I knew that voice, but I didn't want to believe it.

The alley cut through to the next street but halfway it broke off to another alleyway, giving it a T shape. That's where the voice echoed.

She didn't wait to see if I'd follow her voice down the

alley. Your mom swayed into view, dancing to the sound of her own voice. The rumble of the headache seeped into my jaw, clamping it shut.

Her back was turned to me as she shuffled her feet from side to side. Her dancing was better than the last time I saw her stumbling alone in the backyard after your funeral. An invisible partner spun her. Eyes closed, she laughed like a child. Then the invisible partner dipped her, and suspended in the air like that, she opened her eyes and looked at me.

"Oh, don't look so shocked," she said.

She curtsied to the empty space beside her. Something was wrong with her face. It looked like her, but the expressions, the way her face hung on the flesh and bone, it was like a different lattice held it all in place.

The pressure bled out from my jaw and into my clenched teeth. I kept blinking because of how shaky my vision was getting.

"You were holding out on me," she said. "All this time, you knew how to bring back Vera. You made me think death was the end."

She made a flourish with her right arm. "I'm whole again."

But it wasn't Diane.

"You're so sure of that," she said, like she'd heard the thought. "You barely knew me, just like you barely knew Vera."

I wasn't all that sure I could even talk. My whole body

was a flexed muscle. I could hear the molars at the back of my mouth grinding together. I smelled the bone on bone.

"I still remember when she broke up with you," she said, the brunt of her stare pushing down on me. "It was the happiest day of my life. You held her back. She was sick of you being so antisocial, so afraid to do what you wanted. She was better than you. Then your pathetic mother had to get cancer."

My fists curled into themselves. My whole skeleton felt like it was thrashing inside me. A warm trail of blood flowed down my nostril.

"Do you remember begging her to take you back at the hospital?" she said. The sound of her voice was getting heavier. "She went to see your mother and you cornered her in the hall and cried and cried. What else was she going to do? Say no?"

Diane's eyes rolled into the back of her head, and Dr. Jacobson's eel eyes rolled into the sockets. "If she never took you back, she'd still be alive."

The ringing intensified in my ears, and then something gave. White light filled my eyes and something warm filled my mouth. I could move again and I staggered from the alley, collapsing against a building and using it to prop myself up. I got to the curb and pitched forward, letting the contents of my mouth spill between two parked cars. Blood splattered on the asphalt, followed by the skipping sound of teeth, followed by the wet plop of a piece of my tongue hitting the ground.

———

"Christ, kid. What were you chewing on, the curb?"

The dentist moved the overhead light away. He was hunched over and squinting into my mouth. I was lying in an operating chair fully reclined while a nurse suctioned the blood and saliva out of my mouth so he could see. He kept reconfiguring the overhead light that swiveled over the chair. I was still swallowing a lot of blood.

The receptionist had run for someone as soon as I walked into the office and left me holding my mouth, blood dripping between my fingers when I tried to talk. In lieu of explaining myself I just fanned money around as proof that I could pay. The other patients sitting in the waiting room dropped the *Highlights* magazines they were reading and pulled their kids away from the coffee table or nudged their partner and nodded at me. The sun was moving across the sky and its rays rolled off a glass building, shining into the office. The glare pooled over my face and this somehow triggered the exposed roots and damaged nerves to writhe in unison. I pictured tentacles thrashing against my gums and the cracked bone that was tearing through my tongue, whatever was left of it. A dentist finally appeared and waved me into the back, expecting me since the emergency room I first went to had called him.

"They made it sound like you bit half your tongue off," he said. "It's not that bad, but I hope you weren't a

Gene Simmons impersonator, because that tip is gone, my friend."

For the surface cracks, craze lines, he called them, the broken cusps, the serious breaks that went all the way from the chewing surface down to the nerve, the damaged pulp and vertical breaks and dead roots, he said they'd have to put me under.

"Not put you *down*," he said, and chuckled, didn't even try to stop when I stayed quiet.

The anesthesiologist walked in next. I nodded through his spiel without really paying any attention. The nurse gave me the suction wand and I periodically ran it along the inside of my cheeks whenever I felt saliva pooling, careful not to close my mouth around it. The lines in my palms were slick with black debris, dead skin from clenching my fists for so long.

The mask fit over my face and within seconds I heard the helicopter blades whooping in my ears, the sound slowing down. Slower.

My eyes opened and I was standing in a courtyard.

It was daytime, warm but not hot. I felt my arms prickling in the sunlight. A strong wind rustled the lush vegetation and flowers around me. I was back on the island where I had met the cook. Since then, he had been busy.

The courtyard was dark, shrouded, except when I looked in the sky there were no clouds, and the sun was missing. The sky was a crisp blue without it, horizon stretching out until it touched the ocean.

On one side of the courtyard was the mossy slope of a mountain. At the other end was a path that disappeared beyond the hedges.

I followed the cobblestones around a stone fountain that was bone-dry. White lace banners billowed along the edges of the path. Music played from somewhere ahead. A harp? Something light and effortless that didn't drown out the din of conversation that I was drawing closer to.

The talking stopped as soon as I appeared. Someone was pouring water into a glass and when he turned, I saw it was the cook. He smiled.

They were all sitting at a long table draped in white linen, immaculate silverware set for each guest. Sitting on one side of the table were my parents, my father in a suit, my mom in a white church dress. Diane was sitting next to them in a strapless gown. Both of her arms were intact. She was petting Brimley as he lapped water out of a silver bowl. In the distance I saw a large country house sitting on a hill, one of those old, palatial English estates you had fantasized about living in, where all we did was drink tea and be witty. I'd wear a tuxedo to dinner and you would wear all your jewelry, and friends would come over dressed in their finest attire to drink brandy and gossip.

On the other side of the table was Dr. Jacobson, and next to him was the cook, seated now. They were all facing me and beaming, absolutely delighted to see me. At the head of the table was an empty chair made up like a throne, gold trim and velvet cushioning.

"The man of the hour," the cook said, extending his arm to the throne-chair. "Join us."

I squeezed my eyes and opened them, trying to force myself awake. I felt my pockets for my phone to look at the time, to ground me, but it wasn't there.

"This isn't real," I said.

Only the cook broke free of the collective gaze. He chuckled and looked to the others, who were still upright and lovingly smiling. His mouth was churning like a cow chewing cud, and I couldn't remember if their plates had already been filled with food, but they were now, fillets of something light and golden, covered in a silky glaze.

"You're absolutely correct," the cook said. "This is more than real. This is beyond reality."

Brimley was lying on the ground and he got up and sauntered over to me. The end of the tablecloth flapped from the swing of his big tail. He turned his body to press himself against my knees. He craned his head back, licking the air, his orca tongue trying to get to my face.

The cook wiped his mouth with a cloth napkin. "It's not like there, where they die and their absence leaves a void. And everything hurts, and everything aches and bad thoughts manifest themselves, random moods rising of their own accord. Where any joy is laced with fatigue. Only happiness-pain. Love-suffering. Here, everyone's whole again."

Diane waved with the hand that had been sucked into Dr. Jacobson's face. Dr. Jacobson's eyes were back in his head and intact. Brimley didn't have zipper teeth stretched behind his neck. The orange powder staining his snout was gone.

"Where's Vera?"

The cook stood up and excused himself from the table. "I can take you to her."

"She's here?" The desperation in my voice scared me.

"They're all here. They've been waiting a long time. The banquet could never start without you."

"Me?"

Brimley shifted from under my hands and moved to the cook, wagging his tail as the cook ruffled the hair on his neck.

"Yes, you." His eyes widened, a deep breath in and then out. He looked at me like I was wasting so much potential. "You've walked into a party only to realize you are the party. The only reason I invited all these people was because I hoped you would come."

"We've missed you," my mom said.

My dad raised his glass for me to see. "Look. Water. I don't have to drink anymore."

Something was forming inside me, gathering shape with each rotation. I didn't want the cook to hear it, so I pushed the thought as far away as I could, deep into the recesses of my mind, refusing to accept it. Except it kept pushing forward, demanding to be thought of, admitted, said out loud, and when I thought I would scream, my lips and throat and teeth pushed together and made these words: "I miss her so much."

Everyone at the table gasped, surprised. And then their rigid postures dissolved and they looked relieved. They laughed the way people do after a jump-scare they didn't expect. My parents hugged. Your mother covered her mouth, proud of something I couldn't decipher. The cook sighed as if that was it. I had done it, whatever *it* was. He craned his head back and exposed his neck and took a deep breath, and I watched the muscles in his throat disassemble the air for the body's larger purpose. Diane was laughing so hard her head hung over the back of her chair, the far molars in her mouth showing. A cacophony of cackles, everyone laughing and laughing like they couldn't control themselves. My father collapsed to the floor, holding his stomach. His eyes and tongue bulged out of his head. Their collective shrieks grated the inside of my skull.

The cook approached me and clapped a hand on my shoulder. "I know you do. That's why we're here."

He pressed my head gently against his chest, and I closed my eyes. His embrace felt strange. A thick, fibrous body pressed against me, viscous and rigid all at once, the embrace of a cicada dipped in wax. Lifeless and indestructible. On a deeper, vestigial level, where the cook and I were beginning to draw closer, I knew this meant he could never be destroyed, only delayed.

"Who are you?"

His long, spindly fingers caressed my cheek. "It doesn't matter. I was called."

"Out of the flux?"

He didn't answer.

"Why are you doing this?"

His whisper tickled the inside part of my ear. "She's waiting for you. Go to her."

When I opened my eyes, he looked like the cook again. He led me down a narrow path that descended farther along the mountainside until we reached the bottom. We were at the base of the jetty. The sun was absent, but something else, something powerful, was rising above the horizon, its light flaring against the ocean ripples.

At the end of the jetty, blotting out the source, was the wall.

I was overcome with the knowledge that we were standing at the end of the universe. We were on the edge of everything known, the veil drawn thin here—even the light that flared over the horizon and met my eyes, its constituent particles barely held together.

The metallic aftertaste was back. So were the debilitating waves of grief and surrender. If I closed my eyes, I saw a fist surrounded by empty black space. It was gripped around something at the center of my being, and I could just let go and be with you. The fist was trembling, struggling to hold on. Out of the darkness, another hand appeared and slithered up the fist's wrist, sliding over its white knuckles like a glove. Prying the hand open.

I didn't walk. The feet *told* me they were walking, drawn to the wall despite me not wanting to go. They moved from one rock to the next, slabs of onyx, volcanic glass, glistening out of the churning water. It was the feeling from the train platform. Like I was being pulled back from the screen of reality into an incomprehensible emptiness, something else taking my place. *Go to her.* What I knew about the wall had fallen away, leaving only the kernel, the marrow of my unbearable sorrow. Something of me evaporated. Something else remained. The wall loomed and I bowed in its shade, reduced to my most elemental existence. *Pull me out of the wall.* My arm reached out as a voice played in my ear, the voice unfolding a story, the oldest story, the walled garden, the caged paradise, and the eternal fear of being breached. I touched the wall and instead of feeling the slick stone, my fingers sank into the rock and mud and moss, and the cold grasp of someone waiting on the other side latched around my wrist, pulling me into the wall, and I could only look back to realize she was so far behind me. Beyond me. She's gone she's gone she's gone she's

I woke up in the dentist chair, upright, my entire mouth numb and full of sterile sponges.

"There he is," a voice said. The dentist appeared and sat on a stool facing me. "Take a second to get your bearings."

The high from the nitrous was still coursing through

me, echoing his words into nonsense, turning the hiss of a machine into music, but I was lucid enough to feel something was off. The dream was still fresh in my mind, and I kept repeating its details over and over so I wouldn't forget. I patted my pockets and felt my phone, my wallet, the cabin keys I was still carrying with me, but I kept going over the pockets again. The dentist looked suspicious, grinning up at me.

"How you feeling?"

Did I wake up to him going through my pockets? Was my wedding band originally this high up on my finger? I felt like something was missing. Something had been taken from me, but I couldn't figure out what.

"Nothing," I told him. The word sounded like it was pushed through a pillow. My voice was heavy and the word came out like mixed cement. "Just weird dreams." My mouth was packed with gauze.

He cocked his head. "Dreams? That's new. Most people wake up and assume the surgery hasn't happened yet. The consciousness just goes in and out that fast. No one's ever mentioned dreams."

The hotel upgraded my stay into one of their penthouse suites with elaborate moldings and wainscoting, extravagant wood furniture and dark curtains, a wine-colored carpet. I wasn't exactly sure why, but I didn't stop them either. Maybe it had to do with the large tips I was giving the cleaning staff for new pillows. They would swap out the damp, bitter-smelling pillows for dry, fresh ones. I'd wait in the lobby as they turned down the room and watch the video I'd taken of myself sleeping, the volume muted because of how loud I had been weeping, thrashing in the covers but somehow not waking up.

The suite overlooked Lake Shore Drive and its two seg-mented worms of fluorescent lights, one white and one red, squirming in opposite directions. Crowds of people packed onto the sidewalks, and from this high up the tour groups with matching red shirts looked like tumors, the street traffic like rivers of red and white blood cells.

The day of my flight came and went. The morning started with a calendar alert, then an email with my e-ticket, followed a few hours later by a text message from the airline saying I still needed to check in before I could board.

I was actually up before the first alert. I took a shower and shaved, popped a couple Vicodin. I washed my mouth with a cup of warm water and salt because it was still too sore to brush.

My luggage was packed, sitting on the edge of the bed, along with my change of clothes. I turned on the TV and opened the curtains. The lake looked like fish scales under the morning sky. When I turned to leave, my legs jerked at the knees, but my feet stayed rooted to the ground. Before I knew it, every joint had locked into place. It was all of me frozen in front of the window. I screamed but the sound only volleyed between my ears.

I watched the sun rise, the full brunt of its heat searing my face. A cosmic time lapse played outside the window. Night fluttering into day, day lapsing back into night again within a few minutes. The only thing I could do was close my eyes, except doing so would trigger memories of us. Our wedding night. The first time we made love. Each memory played like a movie, me sitting in an empty theater, watching my face on the screen twist and contort into something else, something not me. The face relaxed into the cook's face. You marrying the cook. The cook making love to you.

Someone was standing behind me. I could see them in the reflection of the window. It could only be the cook, but it wasn't his usual form. The shape was dark, as black as space, and slender, threadlike appendages began to push out of his body, hundreds of these antennae encircling him like an aura. I wanted to scream but the television behind me started flipping through channels until it stopped on an airing of *2001: A Space Odyssey*. HAL's unfeeling voice filled the room. "Look Dave, I can see you're really upset about this. I honestly think you ought to sit down calmly—"

My legs jerked backward. The backs of my knees hit the bed and my ass suddenly dropped to the mattress.

"—take a stress pill—"

My good hand slammed against the lamp on the nightstand and snatched the Vicodin bottle before it rolled off the table. My head craned back and the hand popped one, two, three, four, five pills into my mouth. When you don't control the muscles to swallow, it feels like a python is in your throat.

"—and think things over," HAL said. "I know I've made some very poor decisions recently, but I can give you my complete assurance that my work will be back to normal. I've still got the greatest enthusiasm and confidence in the mission. And I want to help you."

I fell back on the bed, and into a deeper darkness.

In the dreams, my point of view was disconnected from my body, so instead of the actor, I was the director on the dolly crane, watching myself walk down a wet sidewalk at night, head lowered with a hood hiding my face, hands in pockets.

To call myself the director makes it sound like I had some kind of control over what was happening. But I was an observer, the camera itself, forced to watch.

I turned onto a side street where the houses clustered together, and gently pushed open a wrought-iron gate to one building, descending the stone steps to its garden unit. My body just stood there, but my camera POV continued, casting a shadow on the front door. The next thing I saw was the garden unit's interior, the sofa and crushed food wrappers, the stacks of magazines and discarded children's toys. To the left of the kitchen was an open doorway. A bedroom.

A perfect lump of a person was hiding under the blanket. A hand I suddenly realized was my own pulled on a corner of the blanket from the foot of the bed. The blanket slowly slid off the lump, revealing Fidelia Marroquín curled into the fetal position, her hands blocking her face.

"Qué quieres?" she said. Her voice was like a little girl's.

The voice coming out of my mouth was not mine. It was Dr. Jacobson's. It was Diane's voice in the alley. It was the sound of vocal cords being thrummed, the body as an instrument.

"Sabes con quién hablas?" the voice said.

From behind her trembling hands, she nodded.

"Por favor," Fidelia said, her entire body shaking, "no quiero morir."

"No te preocupes," the voice said. "El cielo te espera. Aprenderás a llamarlo así."

In the second dream, I was trapped against a hard surface, struggling to breathe.

"Wait," I heard a muffled voice say. "Do you hear that?"

"Yeah," a woman said. "I think it's coming from inside the wall."

Something pulled on me and drew me down into a weightless ether. I was tumbling end over end. When the feeling stopped, I was standing in our living room, but the furniture was different. Framed photos of a young white couple covered the walls. I took a step forward and the floorboards creaked.

The white guy in the photos appeared out of the hallway in a T-shirt and boxers, a baseball bat cocked behind his head. I took another step forward, the floorboards creaked, and he looked at the spot where I stood, but he didn't see me. I looked down and saw I had no body. He kept inching forward, walking through me, and when he did he shook all over and called to his wife, telling her he'd found another cold spot. I moved into the second bedroom where the wife was standing next to a crib and keeping an eye on the doorway. I peeked into the crib and saw their baby sleeping. On top of the dresser was an Itza softly playing a lullaby.

It was barely noon and the line for visitors at the Cook County Jail snaked out of the main office and down the sidewalk. I was surprised when the deputy sheriff took my name and the name of the inmate I was there to see, and just ushered me into a line with other visitors going through security. I half expected to get turned away over some law saying the family of victims couldn't visit their offender in jail.

We stood behind bars while all around us noise filled the hall. The deputies called out to one another, other guards barking instructions to us. The buzzing sound of electric doors opening and closing.

There were girlfriends in low-cut shirts sporting tattoos, one name rolling off a jiggling tit. There were elderly parents and crying children and teens with face tattoos and every corner reeked of piss. I had no idea how I had gotten there. Or why.

The chairs and tables in the visiting room were all metal, and we were told to sit and wait for the inmates to arrive.

I sat facing the door. Inmates entered and sat with their families, girlfriends. The tables hummed with conversation. Esteban approached the doorway and looked around, then stopped when his eyes landed on me. I was leaning against the metal back of the chair, legs spread out under the table, hands in my pockets. He was wearing a beige jumpsuit too big for him. He looked like a boy in his dad's work shirt. He turned to the guard standing next to the door and said something. The guard glanced at me and turned, saying something in return.

Esteban walked over and sat down, scooting his chair from the table so as not to accidentally make contact with my legs, which were still splayed out. He looked at his arms crossed over his chest, the small dents in the table, the security cameras stationed in the corners, everywhere but at me. He looked ready to dart out of the room and was clearly bothered with how at ease I seemed to be. I did nothing to change that.

"What do you want?" he finally said.

My mouth wasn't filled with gauze pads anymore, but I still sounded different, coarser, a husk around the words. "I heard the county mediates meetings between the families of victims and the perpetrator to achieve some kind of closure. The perp ends up apologizing and the family forgives him, some kind of restorative justice program, I guess. So here I am."

His knee was bouncing and the tremors rippled through his upper body, wagging his head. "Yeah? Well whatever that is, this ain't it."

I was surprised how calm I felt sitting this close to him. There were so many times I had fantasized about running him over with my car, imagining I had been there on the platform to throw him onto the tracks. And now here he was, fidgeting in his chair, unable to look me in the eyes like a man. Not allowing him to leave seemed to be enough revenge.

"That wasn't much of an apology. You killed my wife."

A head turned from the next table. Esteban looked at them and went back to looking at his reflection bouncing off the table. "I didn't mean to."

"You didn't mean to."

He propped his elbows on the table and picked at his cuticles. He started to say something and then stopped, changed his mind. "I—I think about it every day."

Among the other inmates in beige jumpsuits, Esteban looked out of place. The others had a feral air about them, a sense of wild strung out in their hair and splotchy faces. They stared through their visitors.

Esteban was still a kid, a kid with a big boy bid attached to his name. I wondered if any of the gangs had braced him to join yet. I wondered if bracing him was where it stopped.

"I'm not a bad person," he said.

I was the second sip on a first cup of coffee in the morning. Every part of me felt streamlined, even though I couldn't remember the last time I'd eaten something, or slept without having nightmares that left me more fatigued. A smile spread across my face.

"How's jail treating you? Making friends?"

His head shot up. "What do you want, man?"

"In your testimony you said something about a guy calling your name. That was why you turned, you said." These were just words coming out of my mouth. I was curious to see where they were going.

Esteban was shaking his head. The cuticles on two fingers were bleeding. His head popped up again. "Look, man. I'm sorry. I'm sorry about everything. I didn't mean it, I swear."

I asked him again about hearing his name on the platform. Nothing had shown up on the security cameras, but he claimed there was a guy. "How did he look?" I don't know why I asked that. I reeled back after I said it, patting my mouth like there was a hair on the tip of my tongue.

Esteban's face strained. "Please . . ."

My hands shot back to their sides and I leaned forward, eager to know what had happened. "Look, I believe you didn't kill my wife. You wouldn't believe how I know, but I know. I just need you to confirm something for me. How did he look?"

A small bubble of spit grew at the corner of his mouth, burst. He was holding on as tight as he could, but the facade was starting to chip. I could see it in the way he avoided eye contact, his general body language that was writhing under my stare, his need to get away, the clipped responses he gave that weren't apologies or explanations. That in his head, he was the good guy in this story.

"It was you, man."

"What?"

"You, on the platform."

"That's impossible. I was driving. What is this?" I had a strange taste in my mouth, metallic. I suddenly felt sober, even though I hadn't been drinking. The dream at the dentist's office came back to me. I had put my hand through the wall and something grabbed me. I could still feel the grip of its long, thin fingers, skin like leather, the nails digging into my forearm.

The words hissed out of him. He was doing all he could to keep it together, bearing down like he was meeting something head-on. Gritting his teeth like as soon as he relaxed, he would scatter into millions of marbles. His hand shook, gesturing at his temple. "Your scalp was peeled back. This intense light was on your face. I could see bone.

Your mouth . . . was foaming . . . Blood and . . . teeth
and shit . . . all jagged. You were making this high pitch
whine—"

"Wait," I said, but couldn't follow it up. My hands
were up for some reason. I couldn't string together enough
words to prove how wrong he was.

"Scared the shit out of me," he said, clearing his throat.
"When I had to tell the story again, I told them I saw a guy
standing there bleeding and shit. Threw me off . . ."

"But look at me, I'm fine."

He nodded at the stitches on my head. "Now you are,"
he said, steeling himself to look at me. "Those teeth look
real new."

"I fell," I said, too quick for it to convince him. "You
killed my wife five months ago anyway."

The conviction in his voice didn't sway. "I didn't know
for sure until I saw you in court. I told the public defender
it was you, on the platform. All beat up, but you. All he
did was get me tested for a psych eval."

He shot up out of his chair and the steel legs screeched
across the tile. Everyone at the tables looked and two guards
stepped forward. I waved at them that it was okay.

"Wait," I said again. It was like someone had flashed
a camera in my face. I was disoriented, struggling to follow what he said and refute it at the same time. The only
thing I could manage was asking him what he asked the
guard when he first came in.

"I asked if he saw you, if you were really there." And then Esteban left.

Your stepdad wouldn't answer my calls. I texted him to say I understood if he didn't want to talk to me, but if he could just give me the phone numbers to the people Diane reached out to while we were in Colorado, I would never bother him ever again. He never texted back. There was no one left to tether me to this world.

Someone knocked on the door.

"Who is it?" I said.

"The concierge, sir."

I looked through the peephole. An attractive brunette in a formfitting skirt and blazer was standing next to a waiter who was pushing a cart draped with a white table-cloth. Sitting on top was a bottle of champagne in a bucket of ice, two champagne flutes, and a covered plate. I opened the door.

"Hello, Mr. Alvarez," she said. "I'm Alexis. We spoke earlier."

The waiter wheeled the cart into the room. He pulled the cover off the plate to reveal a bowl of caviar, a plate of crackers, cheese, and what Alexis had to explain was truffle butter.

"I didn't order this," I said.

The waiter opened a black leather wallet that restaurants

normally use to leave the check, except his had a steno book inside, and he flipped a couple pages before saying my room number and name.

"Did we get your order wrong?" Alexis said, scrunching her face to make it seem like the blame was on her, not that I was a crazy guest who'd forgotten his order. "We'll comp this and I can make sure we get you what you wanted instead."

I was still staring at the pad in the waiter's hand. "No, it's fine. Actually, can I have that notepad?"

The waiter turned to Alexis, confused.

"We can bring you up a new one, sir."

I unfolded a roll of cash and handed him two hundred dollars. "This should be enough. And the pen too."

Without looking at Alexis he ripped out the pages with orders and gave me the pad and pen.

"Is there anything else you need?" she said.

I told her I did. I needed matches, a white ceramic bowl, and a white unscented candle. And more paper.

The cemetery gates were closed for the evening. I walked along the residential side of the grounds, where the street-lights were spaced out, leaving sections of dark. It was like walking out of a dream and into the real world. I stuffed the pint of vodka into my jeans and climbed the gate, the metal catching against my cast but I didn't care. My ankles buzzed when I hit the ground on the other side. The shapes of stone crosses, marble gravestones, small mausoleums, were concealed under the shadows of trees. A haze drifted over the grounds.

The soil on Diane's plot still had to settle before they laid her marker. The light traced the curve of your photo etched by a laser onto the marble. Tracing the words *Till We Meet Again*.

The dream I had at the dentist's office popped into my head. It had turned over in my mind so many times before this that it felt more like a memory, a lived-in experience. But when it played back for me at the cemetery, something was encrypted in it. A code was threaded into the details. It was too big for me to understand.

Except you do, I heard the cook say.

I didn't need any more dreams to tell me what I could already feel. Sometimes I closed my eyes and felt it snaking through me, coiling around my spine. Choking out my memories of you until I had to let go of them to stop it from spreading. The more it sank its claws into me, the more I could see its intentions, what it had planned, and my stomach dropped. I can't stop it. I'm not enough.

I love you, Vera. More than either of us knew.

It was only here because it couldn't access wherever it was you were. It had no power there to force its way inside.

He wasn't after existence, but death. The way a tree that grew around power lines would produce seeds that would sprout other trees with mangled shapes, the way pain and tragedy flowed through the branches of my father's family tree, the cook was trying to insinuate himself into life, braid himself into a person, so when that person died the cook would continue in the seed, in the thing that passed on to the next place after a person died, because the cook was tired, so tired of being caught in the flux between worlds.

Other people's dreams of you made me jealous, but now it was your absence that let me know you were maybe okay. You were somewhere else. You were waiting for me, I hoped.

I sat next to your grave and drank, but I didn't feel sad. I was put off by that realization and turned into myself, searching for the cause, alarmed by my coldness, but a warm wave cascaded over me and took me by the hand, and I was back to not caring again. I stared out at the untouched lot of land across from yours, the tall grass swaying to one side from a strong wind. It looked like the grass was undulating, the field alive, and under a bare tree stood a figure draped in darkness, his features hidden except for those serrated white eyes. Something of me evaporated. Something else remained.

You abandoned me, Vera. Everything with Itza, the wall, it was proof of an afterlife, and you left me behind the first chance you got. I had to fend for myself against your greedy family and all those political outlets with agendas, ulterior motives. You could've done something to help me but you never did. But what did I expect from a woman who knew nothing about hard times, who grew up with both her parents, who never had to struggle a day in her fucking life? You were just like your mother and look where that got both of you. Six feet below the ground. And I was alive. Still here, despite everything. *The coalescing moment.* I looked up in the sky and there were two moons.

The cook was standing behind me, his body pressed against mine. "If you feel like you're going to be alone now," he whispered into my ear, "you won't."

"Stop." All at once my joints locked into place. Every muscle and organ trembled under the force we were placing on each other, wrestling for control in the night-black space behind my eyes, where I could feel him worming deeper into the core of whatever made me *me.*

What he said was the same thing you had told me at my mom's funeral. The muscles in my mouth were vibrating when I wrested their control from him.

"Stop using her words."

I felt his presence behind me like meat hooks plunging into my flesh, and suddenly my feet were leaving the ground, and I was hanging over yours and Diane's graves.

Calmado, venado. My dad's voice echoed out of the ether inside me. *It was never going to be any other way. But we got Fidelia, didn't we? We got that bitch for siccing him on you.*

The taste of spoiled deli meat filled my mouth, and I gagged at the memory of what we did to the old woman.

"And going to see Esteban? Why?"

You needed to see how many lives you've ruined. You couldn't go your whole life without seeing the victims left in your wake, in this family's wake. We're cursed, mijo. And all of our sins flow through you. You keep them alive. But in the darkness we can be redeemed. He wanted to show you. He has always been with you, the old woman's door just made it easier.

I heard the zipper to my pants lower, but my head was locked facing the sky. My consciousness fractured. Hidden behind the stars were terrible truths, a kaleidoscope of nightmares, and beyond them, I saw the shape of a mask, light leaking around its edges.

When I could finally look down I saw my dick was out and I was pissing on your grave. I managed to pinch off the stream and fell to the ground. Curled and weeping on the grass, that night in your hospital room came back to me, the priest on the television saying the point of possession was to make us despair. To see ourselves as animal and ugly. It was hard to see myself any other way.

My hands were still shaking by the time I made it back to the hotel. A group of men and women around my age passed me in the lobby. They looked like out-of-towners dressed in their going-out clothes. A beautiful brunette in a black dress turned to me and I almost collided against the wall to keep our arms from grazing. The front desk clerk was helping an old couple with something, the woman with white hair and a floor-length fur coat. I felt unclean.

In the elevator I kept my eyes down, staring at the recessed lighting above me that was reflected on the floor. When I closed my eyes I saw a grid that went on forever. I saw the malign geometries of constellations.

Mirrors wrapped around the walls of the elevator, so on either side of me were reflections of other elevator cabins with other Thiagos staring at their feet. I didn't look too far out of my peripherals, just enough to see the other Thiagos turn away from the ground to look at me. The doors opened on my floor and I ran to my room, fumbled with the key card until it slid in the slot and the light turned green.

One of those old record players with the brass horn was sitting on the coffee table. The needle traced out a brooding, painful song.

Alexis answered on the first ring. "Enjoying the gramophone?"

"Yeah," I said. What did it matter if I ordered it or not? "Did you get my candle and bowl?"

"As a matter of fact we did, Mr. Alvarez. We're a little busy right now but as soon as one of my—"

"I'm sorry but it's really important that I get that stuff now."

"Sure," she said, paused. "I'll bring it up right now."

I popped open the bottle of champagne. I swallowed all the Vicodin I had left.

Maybe all I have to do is pick a time and say, This is the end. Maybe what qualifies as the end is where I choose to end it.

No end. No end.

As soon as Alexis arrives, I'm burning these pages. Then I'm going to fill the tub with warm water and rest until I slip away and my borders dissolve, like cocoa powder in warm milk. I'll be dead, but the cook will lose. How was this for giving myself over?

It's already over.

I thought I was done apologizing to you, telling you how many times I messed up. But this is the way I have to do it. It's all my fault.

If these waves of Vicodin are any kind of predictor, at least it won't be painful. *The veil is drawn thin here.* And the music is silk in the air, wrapped around Thiago's neck and hands—*the darkness blinds.*

—no—

The darkness washes away.

She's knocking at the door, but when Thiago looks up from the pages, all he sees is stone, moss, the mire of raw earth. It envelops him whole. Only in the darkness are we ever made whole.

There.

There.

The coalescing moment where we became singular.

He claims his seat at the table, among their grating shrieks and yowls, and his mewling carries to the shore, as will yours, as they always have, lapped at by an ocean of flux.

SAHARA ITZA QUICK-START GUIDE

Welcome to ITZA

Sahara is excited to introduce your newest household helper, Itza! Manage alarms, music, shopping lists, and so much more.*

Getting to Know ITZA

Itza is the world's most advanced smart speaker, and she answers only to you! Say Itza's name to "wake" her, and she will play music, make calls, send and receive messages, update you on the latest headlines, sports scores, weather—instantly. All you have to do is ask!

Home

Don't forget about your other smart devices. Itza plays nice, we swear! Ask Itza to dim the lights, adjust the thermostat, start the coffee maker, turn on the TV, even lock the doors. There's nothing she can't access!

Always Improving and Learning

With each use, Itza gets smarter, until you can't remember what you did without her. Every request you make helps her learn your speech patterns, verbal tics, vocabulary, and personal preferences. And because Itza is always connected, updates are delivered automatically. She's there whether you see her, there whether you need her.

What Are You Waiting For?

Set up your voice profile through the Itza app, available for iPhone and Android through the pull me out of the wall.

*Sahara manages and records audio, exchanges, and other information in the cloud to optimize overall services. By checking "Accept," you agree to Sahara's terms and conditions.

Pull me out of the wall
Pull me out of the wall
Pull me out of the wall
Pull me out of the wall
Pull me out of the wall
Pull me out of the wall
Pull me out of the wall
Pull me out of the wall
Pull me out of the wall
Pull me out of the wall
Pull me out of the wall
Pull me out of the wall
Pull me out of the wall
Pull me out of the wall
Pull me out of the wall
Pull me out of the wall
Pull me out of the wall
Pull me out of the wall
Pull me out of the wall
Pull me out of the wall
Pull me out of the wall
Pull me out of the wall
Pull me out of the wall
Pull me out of the wall
Pull me out of the wall
Pull me out of the wall
Pull me out of the wall
Pull me out of the wall

Pull me out of the wall
Pull me out of the wall
Pull me out of the wall
Pull me out of the wall
Pull me out of the wall
Pull me out of the wall
Pull me out of the wall
Pull me out of the wall
Pull me out of the wall
Pull me out of the wall
Pull me out of the wall
Pull me out of the wall
Pull me out of the wall
Pull me out of the wall
Pull me out of the wall
Pull me out of the wall
Pull me out of the wall
Pull me out of the wall
Pull me out of the wall
Pull me out of the wall
Pull me out of the wall
Pull me out of the wall
Pull me out of the wall
Pull me out of the wall
Pull me out of the wall
Pull me out of the wall
Pull me out of the wall
Pull me out of the wall

Pull me out of the wall   Pull me out of the wall
Pull me out of the wall   Pull me out of the wall
Pull me out of the wall   Pull me out of the wall
Pull me out of the wall   Pull me out of the wall
Pull me out of the wall   Pull me out of the wall
Pull me out of the wall   Pull me out of the wall
Pull me out of the wall   Pull me out of the wall
Pull me out of the wall   Pull me out of the wall
Pull me out of the wall   Pull me out of the wall
Pull me out of the wall   Pull me out of the wall
Pull me out of the wall   Pull me out of the wall
Pull me out of the wall   Pull me out of the wall
Pull me out of the wall   Pull me out of the wall
Pull me out of the wall   Pull me out of the wall
Pull me out of the wall   Pull me out of the wall
Pull me out of the wall   Pull me out of the wall
Pull me out of the wall   Pull me out of the wall
Pull me out of the wall   Pull me out of the wall
Pull me out of the wall   Pull me out of the wall
Pull me out of the wall   Pull me out of the wall
Pull me out of the wall   Pull me out of the wall
Pull me out of the wall   Pull me out of the wall
Pull me out of the wall   Pull me out of the wall
Pull me out of the wall   Pull me out of the wall
Pull me out of the wall   Pull me out of the wall
Pull me out of the wall   Pull me out of the wall
Pull me out of the wall   Pull me out of the wall
Pull me out of the wall   Pull me out of the wall
Pull me out of the wall   Pull me out of the wall

ACKNOWLEDGMENTS

I don't think I'll ever be able to thank her enough, but this is a start: thank you to my agent, Annie Bomke, for seeing the potential in this book and taking a chance on me, or what I perceived as a chance. Thank you to my editor, Daphne Durham, for all the invaluable work she put into this book. All she ever did was make it better, creepier, and I would trust her instincts even in a zombie apocalypse. Thank you to Lydia Zoells for her time and involvement and for bringing this book across the finish line. Thank you to MCD for bringing me into the fold. I still can't believe I'm lucky enough to be here. Thank you to Richard Thomas, Jamey Bradbury, Paul Tremblay, Andy Davidson, and Brian Evenson for their kind words. I need to mention Sara Wood for her amazing cover design, and Howie Wonder for his hypnotizing artwork. If we ever meet in person, whatever your vices, I'm buying. Special thanks to Abby Kagan for the book's beautiful interior design.

I wrote this book as a way of dealing with my grief, but I don't get that idea without reading John Langan's *The Fisherman* and Joan Didion's *The Year of Magical Thinking*, and rereading Sara Gran's *Come Closer* for the fourth time. Bret Easton Ellis's *Lunar Park* is in there too. Reading their work helped me when writing felt frivolous. And when it was too painful to do even that, I had the Cranberries, the xx, *808s & Heartbreak*, *Downton Abbey*, and Patton Oswalt's comedy special *Annihilation*. I have to also include Stephen Graham Jones's short story "The Dead Are Not," for devastating me in the hospice parking lot. And while I'm at it, thank you to Stephen Graham Jones, period. All I'm ever doing is trying to get to his level.

This may sound weird, but I hope my family finds some comfort in this story. To my brother, Miguel, this book doesn't make me think I'm an authority on what you've gone through. I could only write from my own perspective. To Kayla, Kane, Kaleb, and Kasey, I am in awe of your resilience and light. Keep going. To my comadre, Charlene, thank you for showing me what it means to really be someone's friend.

Thank you to my mom and dad for everything they've done for me.

Thank you to my wife, Monse, who read this book before anyone else, and who cuddles with the dogs because I can't write like that. Obviously, you inspire me. There is no me without you. Let's order pizza.

And so, Carol. This book doesn't exist without you, and I'd like to think you'd take credit for it, telling people it was *your* book, how I couldn't get one published without you. Thank you for my niece and nephews. Thank you for always being yourself. Whatever of you is in this book, there's more in my head, even more in your husband and children, in Jonathan, the Luques, your comadres, your students, your brothers and parents, and on and on. May we never do you justice. May there always be more to say.